*after*DEATH

a first novel

by

M. Aalis White

This is a work of fiction. Names, characters, places, and incidents either are the product of the author's imagination or are used fictitiously. Any resemblance to actual persons, living or dead, events, or locales is entirely coincidental.

Copyright © 2019 by M. Aalis White

All rights reserved. No part of this book may be
reproduced or used in any manner without written
permission of the copyright owner except for the use of
quotations in a book review.

First paperback edition September 2019

ISBN 978-0-578-58577-2

Published by

nothingmuse ink
4407 cisco valley drive, round rock, texas 78664
www.nothingmuseink.com

*after*DEATH

CHAPTER ONE

Benjamin Asher Nimitz exits his office, adjusts his coat against the October cold, and walks briskly down a busy city street. He takes his usual path, although today his pace is heavier and quicker than usual. Within a few blocks, he arrives at his destination: a high-end brownstone. He walks up the front steps and rings the bell. The door is opened by a butler who removes Nimitz's coat and ushers him into the home.

"Good evening, Mr. Nimitz, sir," the butler greets him.

"Good evening," Nimitz responds politely.

"If you will follow me. It is her wish that you be led to her rooms," the butler informs him as they proceed up the stairs.

Nimitz enters a dimly lit bedroom. His client, Mrs. Greyson, is under blankets in a large wooden-framed bed with her head slightly propped up by pillows. Several family members are gathered around her. Mrs. Greyson's breaths are shallow and raspy. Her doctor is monitoring the medical equipment attached to her. He motions for Nimitz to come closer while also indicating that the family members need to exit the room to allow Nimitz and his client some privacy. The family complies.

Armed with pen and legal pad, Nimitz takes a seat near the bed and leans in as Mrs. Greyson whispers to him her instructions on changing her will. Nimitz quickly takes notes. When Mrs. Greyson is done, Nimitz moves to an exquisite wooden desk across the room so that he can make the proper adjustments. Every few seconds, his client takes a deep, troubling breath, causing Nimitz to pause his writing and look over his shoulder at her before returning to his work. Once completed, he goes to the door, opens it, and motions for the doctor and family members to return.

As he crosses back to the desk, Nimitz notices a woman in the opposite corner of the room. She is standing to the right side of the bed, but closer to the wall and out of the way. She is silent. Nimitz is puzzled by her appearance as he cannot recall her being in the room before. He watches as the woman walks over to Mrs. Greyson, bends down, and whispers into her ear. His focus is broken as Mrs. Greyson takes her last breath. Her family huddles together around her, crying softly. Nimitz looks back at the woman, who notices him looking at her and appears slightly surprised. She looks at Nimitz as she lifts her hand, placing one finger over her mouth in the universal symbol of "shhhh", and then disappears.

Nimitz excuses himself from the room, descends the stairs, takes his coat from the butler, and exits the brownstone. He stops on the stoop and stands in the crisp, autumn air, confused. *What just happened? Am I crazy? No, no mental illness in my family. None.* He starts walking home, his footsteps deliberate but aimless. Something is different. He takes a different route, stopping by the park to people watch. He is smiling. Still confused about what just happened, he knows it was something special. He knows something in him has been changed.

***

Nimitz is walking to work one morning in January. Despite not having found any evidence of the woman in his client's papers, Nimitz has not stopped thinking about her. Light snow is falling and he is bundled against the elements, walking with his head down. Suddenly he stops walking and looks straight ahead. He starts walking faster and turns a corner. Flashing lights, a crowd, and emergency personnel cause him to stop abruptly. He is about to turn around when he sees her. She is standing completely still as people bustle around her. Nimitz is frozen in place as he stares at her. She turns to meet his eyes and makes the same "shhhh" motion with her finger to her lips. This time, though, Nimitz notices a small smile on her face and even what he believes to be a blush upon her cheek, however brief. He smiles back to her, his cheeks red, and he gives a small wave in her direction. She is wearing a handsome grey dress that gives her the appearance of a librarian. Her long dark hair is neatly fastened in a loose chignon.

    As the emergency personnel load a young man into the ambulance, she disappears. This time Nimitz rushes into the fray to give chase, but he cannot find any trace of her. Furthermore, it appears that no one else saw her. Nimitz shakes his head, shivers all over, and hesitantly starts walking to work again. *Ghost? Is she a ghost?* Nimitz doesn't believe in ghosts. *What the hell is happening?*

After work, Nimitz makes his way to a restaurant downtown. He steps into the darkened foyer and takes a seat in the waiting area when he realizes he is the first to arrive. The events of the morning walk to work are still prevalent on his mind as he waits for the rest of his party. Jeanne and Heather are the first ones to arrive. They almost always are since they live within a few blocks of the restaurant and Nimitz and his friends always meet up at this restaurant when they have their get togethers. They walk in laughing, arm in arm. Nimitz enjoys being in their company because they are the closest thing he has to family and, despite his preoccupation with the events of the morning, this evening is no different.

"Benji!" They yell out in unison as they drape their arms around him and hug him. Nimitz kisses each cheek in succession.

"Of course, you're on time. Where are those bastards? We thought we were going to be the last ones to get here." Heather looks around the restaurant.

"You're never the last ones to get here," Nimitz smirks.

"Jeanne was running late getting home. Something came up last minute…"

"Heather, shush! I told you I didn't want to make a big deal out of it!" Jeanne playfully lays her hand over Heather's mouth. Nimitz looks on in amused bewilderment.

"She made partner!" Heather blurts after wresting Jeanne's hand away from her lips.

"Oh my goodness! Jeanne, that's amazing! Congratulations!" Nimitz grabs Jeanne and plants a big kiss on her cheek and hugs her enthusiastically.

"What's amazing?" A tall, broad shouldered blonde man walks up behind Heather and places his arm over her shoulder.

"Hayden! Jeanne made partner!"

"Damnit, Heather! Are you going to let *me* actually tell anyone *my* big news?"

"I'm sorry, sweetie. I'm just so proud of you and happy for you." Heather leans in and gives Jeanne a kiss then softly pushes her dark blonde hair out of her face. "Plus, this means we can start our family."

"Well, then, it looks like we've got things to celebrate. Shit, I thought tonight was just going to be the standard cocktails and complaints bullshit session we normally have! Congrats, Jeanne."

"Thanks, Hayden." Jeanne embraces him. "Where are Ferrol and Dean?"

"They'll be along shortly. Traffic."

"Good. I'm starved!" Heather announces as she glances over at Nimitz, who is quieter than usual. She slips to his side. "You okay, Benji?"

Heather and Jeanne are the only people in the world who call Nimitz by the nickname. Other than his parents, but they are no longer alive. Nimitz likes that they call him Benji. He gives a soft smile at Heather and mumbles that he is okay, "I'm just a little preoccupied. And tired."

"What's got you preoccupied? Something going on at work?"

"Jeez, Heather, you are the nosiest damned woman I know. Have been since I've known you. Pretty sure I only married you to keep you from snooping into even more of my past!" Jeanne smirks in Heather's direction.

"That's a damned shame, then! I would have married you for your body, baby!" A ginger-haired man of average height says as he sidles up behind Heather, adjusting his glasses. Next to him stands another man with a dancer's build.

"It's about time!" Hayden booms over the noise of the group and the restaurant. "Dean, Ferrol, good to see you both."

"Are we all here?" Ferrol asks rhetorically, taking a mental head count before informing the maître d' they were ready to be seated. "Our table's ready, ladies and gents."

"Thanks, Ferrol, sweetie," Heather coos as the group follows the maître d' to a table in one of the more private enclaves. The men all stand until Jeanne and Heather are seated.

"I swear, Heath, what would we do without these men in our lives?" Jeanne jokes.

"I know. Almost makes me wish we weren't lesbians." Heather retorts.

"Bite your tongue! Or mine!"

"One of these days, Dean, some woman is going to call you out on that bullshit and your face is going to turn the same shade of red as your hair," Hayden warns playfully and the whole table erupts in laughter.

Nimitz has known Jeanne and Heather since childhood. He and Heather would sneak innocent kisses on the lips when they were kids. Jeanne was one of his first running buddies. They played basketball, skateboarded, and spent hours talking about life, family, school, and the future. One would think that Nimitz would have been jealous when Jeanne and Heather started dating each other in high school, but he was happy for them. He felt they were great together and loved seeing them still happy and in love all these years later. He met Hayden in college. They both attended law school together as well, which is where they met Dean. Ferrol had gone to college with Heather at Tulane University in New Orleans. He was transferred to New York with his job over a decade ago and had fallen in with their group quite nicely. He was a bit more reserved and quieter than the others which was why Nimitz identified with him more closely than the rest of the group. These days he spent more time with Ferrol than anyone else in the group.

    The friends laugh and talk for a few hours over dinner and drinks. This is a monthly event in which they engage. Life, work, relationships, and distance across the city have made it almost impossible to meet up for anything other than a monthly meeting so they make it a priority. Tonight, Hayden's wife is unable to attend because she is home with the kids who both have the flu. Nimitz quietly sips his cocktail, contemplating the people around him, and thinking about the woman.

"There's quiet and there's completely mute, man!" Dean, who has just returned from the restroom, claps his hands down on Nimitz's shoulders and gives him a gentle shake. "What gives?"

"I sure as hell hope you washed your hands," Nimitz quips with a sly smile to everyone's delight.

"Seriously, though," Dean continues unfazed as he returns to his seat, "what's going on? You've been more quiet than usual. Also, I didn't wash my hands. You're welcome."

"It's true," Jeanne and Heather chime in.

"The quiet part," Heather adds. "I'm not entirely sure he's joking about the part where he didn't wash his hands." She winks at Dean.

Everyone quiets and leans in towards Nimitz, waiting for his response.

He takes a long, slow drink of his cocktail, considers the glass. For a brief moment he contemplates telling them about the woman, but he realizes that he wouldn't even know what to say about it all without sounding crazy so he softly says, "Seriously, everyone, it's just boring old work stuff."

"Anything we could possibly help with? I mean, you're not the only lawyer at the table." Hayden offers.

"Yes, I hear one even made partner recently," Ferrol raises his glass a little and tips it at Jeanne with a smile and a wink. She returns the gesture.

"Really, it's nothing, but I appreciate the offers. I'm sure I will have it all figured out within a few days. Please, let us carry on with our celebration." He raises his glass to the table.

The remainder of the dinner carries on in the usual manner. Pockets of serious discussion interspersed with dirty jokes and smartass comments engage the party as they eat their meals, drink their spirits, and enjoy each other's company. At the end of the evening, quips and jokes are shared on the street in front of the restaurant. Hugs, kisses, and handshakes are given before everyone departs towards their homes. Nimitz slowly makes his way to his apartment thinking about the woman and what it might all mean.

By the time he reaches his door, he is exhausted and goes straight to bed, falling asleep almost immediately.

***

Nimitz sits in silence and thought in the dark on a cool April night. He gets up and heads into the kitchen when he realizes he is hungry. He mindlessly reaches into the refrigerator and grabs the first thing he sees which ends up being a bag of grapes. Walking back to his couch, he tosses a few into his mouth. One lodges itself in his throat. Frantically, Nimitz rushes back into the kitchen. He looks around panic stricken trying to recall how to dislodge something from one's throat when one was choking. He knows he needs to Heimlich himself, but how? He focuses on the edge of the kitchen counter and proceeds to ram his sternum against it.

He is becoming dizzy from lack of oxygen when he sees her. Out of the corner of his eye, he sees her. She is different yet again. Her features are softer, and her handsome grey dress is now a little more like the skirt and cardigan outfits that smart girls wore in the 1950s. Nimitz freezes as he watches her walk towards him. She silently studies his face. Then she smirks and shakes her head "no". Nimitz feels a force within him slam his sternum once more against the counter and the guilty grape flies from his throat. He falls to the floor gasping for air, his hands on his chest. He looks wildly around the room for her, but she is nowhere to be found.

Nimitz whispers, "Death".

Laying on the floor of his quiet apartment, with sweat and spittle all over his face and chin, with a half-chomped grape mocking him from under the counter, Nimitz realizes that she isn't a hallucination, ghost, or angel. He realizes that she is death. Nimitz realizes he is smitten with death.

***

Nimitz walks out of a hospital room with his briefcase in hand. His demeanor suddenly changes as he looks down a hall. He heads towards the elevators, pushes the down button, waits, and then gets into the car when the doors open. He steps out of the elevator on the first floor of the hospital and follows the signs for the ER. He walks into the ER and looks around the room.

He sees the woman standing next to a doctor. He cannot see who she is looking at and he doesn't care. He just stares at her, beaming, a broad smile across his face. The woman's stiff posture softens. She looks over her shoulder to Nimitz and, this time, she smiles a real smile. Nimitz walks towards her, opening his mouth to say something to her, when she fades before his eyes. Undaunted, Nimitz walks out of the ER with a smile and a light step. The walk of a man in love.

He hails a taxi from the street in front of the hospital, tells the driver the address, and relaxes back into the seat. The city sounds around him, the pungent odors of traffic, and the irritated mumbling of the driver have no effect on Nimitz's mood or smile as he gazes out the window and daydreams. For a moment, there is a flicker of concern in his eyes before it is shaken away by the braking of the taxi in front of the café. Nimitz pays the driver, grabs his briefcase, and heads into the café to meet Ferrol.

"So, to what do I owe this special, private meeting?" Ferrol teases Nimitz as they greet each other. "Everything alright?"

Nimitz takes a seat at the table, flags down a waitress, orders a coffee, and settles in for what he expects to be a heady conversation.

"Ben," Ferrol looks a Nimitz with a furrowed brow, "you're freaking me out a little, man. What's going on?"

Ferrol is the only person who calls him Ben. Nimitz is comforted by this. He takes a deep breath and looks Ferrol right in his deep brown eyes and announces, "I think I'm going to die soon."

Ferrol chokes out an uneasy laugh at this statement before realizing that Nimitz is completely serious. "What the hell? Are you sick? Why haven't you said anything, Ben? What's going on?"

The waitress brings Nimitz's coffee and asks the men if they want to order any food. They both nod in the negative, so the waitress lays the bill on the edge of the table and walks away. Nimitz takes a long sip of coffee and then addresses Ferrol's questions.

"I am about to tell you some things, some things that might make you believe that I have lost my mind. I can assure you, though, that I am completely sound in my thinking. Before we get into this, I just want you to hear me out. I ask this of you as a friend. As I tell you this, I need for you to keep in mind who I am, who I always have been, what you know of me, and what type of person I am. Are we clear on this?"

Ferrol is completely taken aback by the direct nature of Nimitz's statements. Nimitz has always had a more passive personality, more laid back and soft spoken. This man before Ferrol is very plaintive, commanding, and self-assured in his requests. "Completely clear, Ben."

"Good. Thank you." Nimitz begins telling Ferrol all about the woman. He details every encounter with her exactly how he remembers it happening, including how she has, on more than one occasion, disappeared before his very eyes. He tells Ferrol about the incident with the grape from the previous week. He then pauses for a moment to allow Ferrol to take all of it in before he adds the finishing touch, "I now believe that this woman is, in fact, Death personified. I also believe that I am developing feelings for her or am becoming obsessed with her. Something. I don't know. It's very hard to explain. All I know is that I think of her constantly and I am drawn to places where she appears. I also believe that this all means I will die soon."

Ferrol's jaw drops open slightly and his eyes search Nimitz's for some sign that this is all an elaborate prank. He catches his breath, composes himself, and then contemplates everything he has just heard while repeatedly dunking the tea bag in his already over-steeped cup of tea. He opens his mouth to say something numerous times before closing it again and thinking further on the subject at hand. Nimitz recognizes that his friend is struggling with what he has just been told, so he gently reminds Ferrol, "Remember who I am."

"It's a lot, Ben," Ferrol admits. "I've known you a long time and you are not one to tell wild tales about supernatural experiences. I don't even know your beliefs on such things because you really don't discuss it. So, to be told that you believe you've seen Death in person, fallen in love with Death, and believe that you're about to die is very hard to wrap my mind around."

"I know," Nimitz says quietly.

"You know that I'm going to tell you that this woman is not really Death personified, right?"

"I know that's what you'll say. That's why I wanted to discuss it with you. I knew that you would not hold back with me. I also knew, though, that you would be able to talk it through with me. How would you explain it?"

Ferrol pauses, considering all the information thoughtfully before he speaks. He knows that if he approaches this part of the conversation the wrong way, it could possibly cause irreparable damage to his friendship with Nimitz and, perhaps, to Nimitz's state of mind as well. He fidgets with his tea cup a bit.

"You lost both of your parents within a year of each other and only a couple years ago." Nimitz opens his mouth to respond to this, but Ferrol stops him with an upraised hand. "Hear me out. You asked me how I would explain it, so I am explaining it. There will be time afterwards for your rebuttal. Losing a parent can be devastating. Losing both even more so. I know how close you were to your mom and dad. You first saw this woman at the bedside of a dying client, who then died while you were in the room. There are not a lot of people in this world outside of certain careers that witness people dying. To be in the room when someone takes their last earthly breath is an impactful thing, Ben. I think, and this is going to sound like some New Age bullshit, that you are having an existential crisis of sorts. I think you compartmentalized your mom's death because you felt you needed to be strong for your dad. I think you compartmentalized your dad's death because you didn't know how to process it. You threw yourself into your work. Ben, we didn't see you for months after their deaths. We all understood, but, at the same time, we knew that you needed to let it out and just didn't know it. That's why we pushed so hard to get you back into the monthly dinners. I think being in the room when your client passed threw your brain into a tailspin. On a subconscious level, I think you were reminded of your parents' deaths and it initiated a crisis. I don't think you're crazy. Not by any means. I do think you're finally feeling the grief of your parents' deaths. I think the way your mind is combatting it is by making you see this beautiful woman and causing you to feel love for her. It's a way of accepting your parents' death, of making something beautiful from their loss. You feel like you're going to die because you are feeling that grief on such a fundamental level that it is like a foreboding. You're not seeing death, Ben. You're not in love with death and you're not going to die soon. You're just finally allowing yourself to experience the deaths that you've suppressed. It's okay, Ben," Ferrol puts his hand on Nimitz's. "Lean on us. We can carry you through this. Maybe you should even consider taking a sabbatical from your work. Take a trip. How long has it been since you've gone to Maine? I know that was some place special for you and your parents. A couple of weeks in Maine, communing with their spirits, so to speak, might be just what you need to come to peace with all of it." Ferrol leans back in his chair and smiles softly in Nimitz's direction. "There you go. That's how I explain it. Now, counselor, you have the floor."

Nimitz ponders Ferrol's words for a moment, then concedes that he has valid points. "I understand why you believe what you do. It is so real, though. So very real. I have never felt emotion like this, so strongly. I have never had something manifest before me that doesn't exist in the eyes of others. I have never had said manifestation then disappear before my eyes. In my waking. These weren't dreams. These things happened in broad daylight, in public settings, with other people present. It makes sense, though, that it isn't real. You make a lot of sense. I knew you were the right person to talk to about this because I knew you would be able to contextualize it for me and explain it. Doesn't make it any easier, though, to accept. She was so beautiful, Ferrol. I've never seen someone so beautiful before. And it felt so real to me. I just don't know how to process this. I wanted it, you know? I know that sounds insane, but I wanted her and I wanted this…whatever it was going to be. It's going to be hard to come to terms with the idea that neither is real."

Ferrol senses Nimitz's sadness. He worries his friend won't overcome the original loss because of this new one. "It is real, Ben, just not in the sense that you think. You had to give it context, so your brain created a context for it: a beautiful woman and love. That doesn't make it less real. The emotions you felt, your appreciation for the woman's beauty, your feelings for her, these are all very real because it is your subconscious processing of grief. It is your acceptance of the deaths of your mother and father, as well as that of your client. Accepting their deaths allowed you to move past the negative thoughts you had regarding their loss and move into the happy memories. That's where the beauty and love are from."

"Thanks, Ferrol. One last thing?"

"Anything."

"Please don't mention any of this to anyone. I already get treated much like the baby brother. This would absolutely through me back into diapers as far as Jeanne and Heather would be concerned." Nimitz smiles at him weakly. "You, my friend, are one hell of a therapist."

Ferrol sees through the humor. He knows that Nimitz is still fragile from this conversation, but he also knows that further discussion will only deepen the feeling of loss. "I will consider it as if it were patient confidentiality," he assures Nimitz before he steers him towards lighter topics until they say their goodbyes.

***

Between the first course and the main, Nimitz becomes aware that he is being watched. He snaps his attention back to the table to find six sets of eyes on him.

"I'm sorry," Nimitz is slightly embarrassed. "Did I miss something?"

"Jackie asked if you had gotten a call from her friend, Therese." Hayden motions to his wife who is sitting to his left.

"Oh my, Jackie. I am so sorry. Um, who? Oh! Therese! Oh, yes, now that you mention it, she has called. I left a return message with her assistant. Thank you so much for referring her to me. I appreciate the fact that you thought of me."

"Who else would I think of? You're great at what you do, take excellent care of your clients, and have the most admirable ethics. Of course I would send a friend to you, dear. I must ask, though, are you okay? You seem a bit preoccupied tonight." Jackie's concern sends a ripple of echoes around the table.

"Yeah, man, what gives?" Dean tosses out.

"This isn't the first dinner in recent time that you've taken to the benches on, Nim," Hayden reminds him. "Is everything okay?"

Nimitz leans back in his chair, fidgets with his glass a moment while he considers his words, then confesses, "I think I met someone."

Cheers erupt from the table as glasses are raised in Nimitz's direction. Heather leans over in her chair to plant a kiss on his cheek before Jeanne interrupts the jubilation with a simple question.

"Wait, what do you mean you 'think' you met someone?" The table again falls silent.

"It's complicated."

"No, not really, man," Dean reasons. "Either you met someone or you didn't. There's nothing really complex about that.

"He's gotcha there, Nim," Hayden agrees.

"Spill the details," Jeanne urges.

"Yeah, we've been waiting for this to happen!"

"Jeez, Heath, you make it sound like he's a mutant or something. He's just got discriminating taste. He's selective. Nothing wrong with that." Jeanne turns her attention back to Nimitz. "Tell us everything, Benji."

"The thing is I've seen her a few times, informally. In passing might be more accurate. We've never properly been introduced. I told you, it's complicated."

Hayden and Heather share a surprised glance between them. "Is she married? Is that what it is? Are you seeing her in some sort of situation where she's with her husband or family?" Hayden is talking like a lawyer.

"No," Nimitz replies sheepishly. He does not want to discuss the fact that the woman has disappeared before his eyes. He knows they will mock him relentlessly about it. That's why he had discussed it with Ferrol in private. Nimitz shoots Ferrol an anxious glance. "Can we just leave it at I met someone? I'm not really ready to discuss it further. Please know, though, that I will tell you all about her once I am ready. It's just early right now and I don't want to, I don't know…"

"Jinx it. You don't want to jinx it." Ferrol finishes Nimitz's thought.

Nimitz looks at him, relieved, and nods. He knows it's silly. He knows there's no such thing as a jinx or a curse, but he also knows that he hasn't felt this way in his life and he doesn't want to spoil it. He also knows the pity he will receive if nothing manifests.

"Understood, man," Dean sighs as the others at the table all nod in supportive agreement and dinner wraps up in the usual fashion.

***

Nimitz is walking home. It is Halloween night and there are costumed adults and children everywhere. Nimitz meanders, taking his time, amused by the sights of the holiday. A hooded figure catches his eye. The costume is of death in the traditional sense: black hood and cape, skeleton mask, scythe. The hooded figure walks toward Nimitz and he chuckles to himself at the ridiculousness of the costume.

Nimitz abruptly looks away and starts walking towards his apartment with purpose. He swings opens the door. The sun has now fully set and everything is dark. He enters, throws his briefcase onto the chair, and walks into the dining room where he finds the woman sitting at the table. She stays silent, looking at him with tenderness, as he nervously addresses her.

"I...how did you get...no matter. I've been wanting to meet you. This is crazy. Where are my manners? Would you care for some tea? I will make us each some tea."

He heads into the kitchen and grabs the cord for the electric kettle, his palms dewy. He's shaking with excitement that he is finally meeting her when he hears her speak as he plugs in the kettle.

"Any moment now, darling."

The room jolts and blurs. He is not sure if she is speaking aloud or if she is communicating with him telepathically. His whole body begins to convulse. He is sweating profusely before he vomits. He falls to the floor, legs splayed, hands gripping his chest as he tries to stem the pain. He can see her standing over him. He doesn't think he can trust his vision (or his interpretation of events), but he thinks she looks sad. The last thing he remembers is reaching out to her to try and comfort her.

He can see her blurred form. He can also see himself sprawled out on the floor. She is kneeling next to him. Then she is gone.

Everything goes black.

***

Nimitz, his mind racing in the blackness, thinks to himself, *What is...is this it? Is this what happens? Just nothingness? This can't be the end, can it? I'm still thinking. I mean, I think I'm still thinking. Are my eyes open? Do I still have eyes? A body? Am I really seeing this blackness or is my brain just winding down and these are my final thoughts? What was that story about the man who had been blind since birth? He only sees black? No. He's been blind since birth. He doesn't know what black is. He sees nothing. Am I seeing nothing? Okay, let's calm it down. If this is where and how I will spend eternity, then I think I need to consider some things logically and calm down a bit. Breathe. Wait, do I still breathe? That's neither here nor there. Am I in pain? No. Is it hot? No. Cold? No. Eternity spent within the confines of one's own mind and nothingness. That could be interesting or downright maddening. No way to know how time is passing. No way to know when or how or even if this will ever end. What was the point? Did I seriously fall in love with Death? How would I even know? I've never really been in love before. One thing is for certain: I've never felt the way I felt when I would see her. Never in my life. My life. Was the purpose of seeing Death all those times so that I could come to terms with my own mortality? Is that what happens to everyone? Maybe it wasn't love? Maybe it was just acceptance. Was it? I thought that was how love was supposed to feel, though. That's what movies and books always advertised. That weak in the knees giddy butterflies in the stomach feeling. That feeling of not being able to get someone out of your head. Why haven't I ever been in love? Why wasn't that more prominent in my life? Why didn't I chase love the way others did? What was I waiting for? I guess it doesn't matter now.*

Images flash through Nimitz's mind. He thinks of his mother. His mother was a beautiful woman. He remembers how she would sing him to sleep. She didn't have the best voice, but it was soothing and she sang with conviction at his bedside or when she was rocking him. She would rework the lyrics to include his name when she could. He remembers his father: a tall, thin man who could appear gruff, but was humorous. His father always made his mother laugh. She would comment that it was what made her fall in love with him. Nimitz thinks about his childhood. He thinks about the times his father took them to the coast for a vacation. They camped on the beach, built sandcastles, dug for clams and shells and played in the water.

He thinks about the time Bobby Tisdale hit him in the face with a baseball and his mother thought he was going to lose his front tooth. He thinks about the kiss that Heather had given him when they were in third grade and they were playing hide and seek. She and Nimitz were hiding in the shed behind her house and she kissed him out of nowhere. She kissed him a few times after that, but they were not the passionate kisses of crushes. They were the mischievous, playful kisses of children. Nimitz had experienced other kisses, but none that held any special place in his memory.

He thinks about high school and weekends spent playing role-playing games in Mike Flood's rec room with the other guys. He thinks about college. He spent most of his time studying in the dorm since his roommate pretty much resided with his girlfriend in an off-campus apartment. He had been thankful for that because by the time he had reached college, he had become introverted. Hayden was the only thing that kept Nimitz from being a complete hermit. They would go out for drinks every weekend, play frisbee golf on the quad, or hang out with some other friends at off-campus apartments or outings. Dean joined in that mix in law school. He remembers his graduation from law school. His parents were both there and proud of their son. They took him out for a nice dinner afterwards and discussed job offers that he had received.

He remembers his mother's funeral. She has only been gone for a few years now. Cancer. Sometimes it got people who had never done anything cancerous. Neither of his parents had ever smoked. His mother ate healthy, took excellent care of herself, and did not indulge in junk foods or other possible toxins. Yet cancer still came for her. His father was devastated. Nimitz could tell that his father lost part of his soul, part of who he was, the day his wife died. His humor was dulled after that. He didn't laugh as much. He grew sullen. Within a year of

Nimitz's mother dying, his father passed in his sleep. Nimitz believed his father had been dying since the day his mother did, it just took him a little longer to succumb.

Nimitz thinks about his whole life in this manner. Skipping from memory to memory, watching them play out in his head like a documentary.

How could someone raised by two individuals who were so in love with each other in a house full of love, support, and encouragement, go through an entire life without finding love himself? Why didn't I go to more parties in college, get drunk, and kiss a stranger? Why didn't I take more risks? Put myself out there more? Is this what this is going to be? Eons of me regretting chances not taken in life? I have got to stop thinking like this. This can't be it. There has to be something more. I hope there's something more.

As Nimitz finishes this thought, almost on cue, a small pin prick of light appears. It remains the same size and in the same spot for a few seconds. It then appears to go into hyper drive as it grows rapidly, bigger, wider, and brighter.

Before he can process what is happening, Nimitz finds himself seated in a chair in the center of an all-white circular room. Against the walls are chairs that encircle him with a singular, white-paneled desk in front of them. There are violet-eyed men and women of various ages and races dressed in white robes seated in the chairs. Behind each chair is a white door. Nimitz looks around nervously, supposing this is where he will be judged.

The Council speaks, in unison, "We welcome you, Mr. Benjamin Asher Nimitz. Have you any questions?"

"Who are you? Where am I? I'm dead, right? Is this heaven? Hell? Limbo?" Nimitz explodes with rapid questions.

"Steady, Mr. Nimitz. One at a time. We are here to determine the contents of your Eternity. We are The Council. Where you are is of no consequence since here and there no longer truly exist in your state. Heaven and hell are constructs of the mind. As is limbo. In terms you might understand, your body has expired. Your current state as a soul is post-death. Your soul will have an Eternity, the contents of which will be determined here. Have you any other questions?"

"If I'm dead and only a soul, why do I still have a body? Why do you all have bodies? I don't understand what you mean by the contents of my eternity being determined here. Is this Judgment? Are we here to judge whether I get into heaven or hell? I'm a non-practicing Jew. I mean, I was, but does that matter?" Nimitz asks confusedly.

"You do not have a body, nor do we. What you are seeing is a memory of what you looked like. Your soul projects it as it is something with which you are comfortable. We do not have bodies. Your soul projects us in a manner comfortable to you for our purposes here. There is no judgment. You choose the content of your Eternity. Before you found yourself in our presence, you were in darkness where you entered a stream of consciousness. While in this state, you created your own streaming sequence. By this it is meant that you reviewed your own life in flashes, pictures, memories, emotions. Each individual has his, her, or their own crafted Eternity, the contents of which are determined based on any number of criteria: the type of person he, she, or they was in life, the manner of the soul, the person's memories collected during the streaming sequence, and personal requests."

"So, none of this is real? My body. You. It's all a hallucination?" Nimitz is now utterly confused.

"If that is what you are comfortable with, yes," The Council consents.

Nimitz pauses for a moment, trying to wrap his mind around what is happening. "The manner of the soul?"

"By this it is meant any religious affiliations or belief systems," The Council explains.

"You said personal requests," Nimitz ventures.

"Yes, personal requests are taken into consideration."

"I would like to request that my Eternity be spent with the woman I love."

The Council smiles politely, "That is a popular request. Unfortunately, Eternities cannot be constructed to involve developing, continuing, or future relationships."

"I'm in love with Death." The proclamation fills Nimitz's chest and he takes on the posture of a man who has just discovered his power.

There is hushed but excited muttering among The Council, "It would not be possible to allow your Eternity to involve Death."

Nimitz erupts with frustration, "You said personal requests were taken into consideration!"

"They are, Mr. Nimitz. Your personal request, however, is beyond our scope."

"I don't understand. You keep saying that this Eternity will be constructed, so why can't you construct an Eternity where I am with Death? It's not like I'm asking to be with someone in the living world or to be alive again."

Nimitz's cheeks are flushed and he is breathing deeply. He is shocked and thrilled by this passion coming from him. It is new and electric. It scares him a bit because he has never spoken to anyone or reacted this way to anything like this before.

"Mr. Nimitz! Control yourself. We are not the enemy. We have our own sets of rules by which we must abide. Unfortunately, your request goes beyond the confines of those rules. It has been decided that you are worthy of an Eternity spent on perpetual holiday as a child with your parents in a cottage on the coast of Maine. You are deemed worthy of this Eternity as you were a good person in life, have no specific religious affiliation over your soul, and the memory stood out strong during your streaming sequence."

Nimitz opens his mouth to speak against this determination, but each member of The Council is exiting through the doors behind their chairs. Once the doors are all closed behind them, the floor beneath Nimitz's chair begins to descend with him nervously squirming. The chair stops on the floor of the level below the council room. This new room is softer in warm neutral tones, dimly lit, and smaller. Once the chair stops moving, two orderlies step forward. They are dressed in uniforms: crisp white shirts tucked into white uniform trousers, black belts, and black work boots. Nimitz notices that they also have bright, violet eyes like the members of The Council.

"Please come with us," the first orderly politely requests.

Nimitz nervously queries, "Where are you taking me?"

The second orderly responds, "You are to be outfitted with your Eternity."

"Outfitted? What does that mean? What are you going to do to me? What's going to happen? Will this hurt?"

"Steady, sir," the first orderly coos. "This will not hurt at all. Please come with us."

Nimitz reluctantly follows them, surrendering to his new reality. They leave the small room through a thick metal door and enter a dizzyingly long hallway. The hallway is neutral in color, warm tones, with soft lighting above. On either side of the hallway are rooms with small windows. As they walk down the hall, Nimitz peeks into the rooms and sees different individuals who appear to be floating mid-air and sleeping. They reach a door and stop.

The second orderly opens the door and the first orderly ushers Nimitz into the room. The room is an extension of the hallway: same colors, tones, and lighting. It is a blank space with nothing on the walls except what looks like a control panel. The first orderly looks at Nimitz, indicates a spot in the center of the room and says, "Please stand here."

Nimitz steps into the spot. The first orderly nods to the second orderly who is at the control panel. The orderly presses a button and Nimitz is gently levitated off his feet. He then finds himself floating prone to the floor, hovering about five feet above it. The first orderly nods again to the second, who presses another button. Nimitz relaxes. He is in Maine. He is seven. He can feel the breeze on his skin, smell the ocean, and see his mother and father sitting on the porch of the cottage. He walks to the water's edge and waits for the waves to hit him. As they do, he looks over his shoulder again to his mother and father and smiles. The second orderly presses one last button, lowering the lighting, before both orderlies leave the room, closing the door behind them.

Nimitz and his mother and father are roasting marshmallows over a bonfire on the beach at night. He's playing in the water and the sand. They all go walking down the beach, collecting shells.

Nimitz is alone on the beach. His parents are reading on the porch of the cottage. Nimitz looks up at the rocky shore in the distance. He sees someone standing on the rocks. He cannot make out who it is. The figure is slight, dark, and blurred.

Nimitz is in the water. His parents are sitting in chairs at the water's edge with their feet in the water watching him. He looks out into the ocean and sees someone standing on the water. He squints his eyes, not believing what he is seeing. The figure hovering over the water is the same one he had seen on the rocks. A spark of recognition flickers in his eyes.

He is on the porch. His parents are inside. He sees the figure again standing at the water's edge. This is the closest the figure has been. Still dark, but less blurred, Nimitz can make out that it is a woman. He stands up straight, grips the wooden porch railing tightly, and smiles.

Nimitz opens his eyes in his Eternity room.

CHAPTER TWO

William is pissed off. He looks at his manager and unleashes. "I don't give a shit if the legal crap is in order already or not! We've been working on this for almost a year now and I'll be goddamned if I am going to let some lawyer bullshit put it off. Do whatever you have to do to get it legal before the show ends!"

He pushes his manager out of his way and prepares himself to step onto the stage. His manager, a short, round man with thinning hair and moist forehead and armpits, gets on the phone and starts negotiating legalities. Dramatic TV show theme music plays as an announcer's voice is heard from offstage somewhere in the dark.

"Ladies and gentlemen, please welcome Dr. William Peters, The Deathhunterrrrrr!"

William rushes out onto the stage to the roar of a live audience and thunderous applause. He holds his hands up to quiet the audience as he gets very serious.

"I'm going to keep this short because, tonight on Deathhunter, we are going to be making history. Not only television history, but scientific history. Tonight, we will be crossing over live. We will be summoning Death itself by inducing a Near Death Experience. I will be accompanying our volunteer as he crosses over. I hope to make contact with Death tonight live on this program in an attempt to prove that Near Death Experiences are real and that Death can be captured. Here we go, ladies and gentlemen! Let's cross over and hunt Death!"

The audience responds with more enthusiastic applause and cheers. William walks backstage where he is greeted again by his manager.

"William, there's no way. The lawyers are losing their fucking minds here. You're basically going to kill someone on live TV. Will, they are not going to let it happen. They're going to shut you down before it happens."

William puts his hands on the portly man's shoulders and leans in close to his face, "Your job is to make sure that it ***does*** happen, Jakey. We're going through with this. The volunteer already signed all the paperwork. So did all the crew, the medical personnel, the audience members, everyone. They can go back on it, if they want, after all is said and done, but they signed the fucking paperwork, they know what they're signing up for, and we're gonna give it to 'em! If they even try to go back on it, my lawyers will skewer them. Buckle up, Jakey. It's show time!"

"Okay, Will. Okay. Whatever you say, man," Jake slinks back into the wings defeated. "You're the boss."

"Damn straight, I am. I'm about to become a fucking legend!"

As the announcer explains what is about to happen, curtains part to reveal a sterilized medical room on the stage. The volunteer is already in place on an operating table. He is attached to various medical equipment. Medical personnel are setting up within the sterilized room. William is now on another operating table next to the volunteer's. He is not hooked up to any equipment.

"Ladies and gentlemen, we ask for complete silence," the announcer's voice is a deep whisper. "For our purposes tonight, a sterilized medical room has been created on the stage. This room follows all medical guidelines and has been approved by our staff doctor. This room has been created to limit any possibilities of outside contamination during the induction of the Near-Death Experience. The volunteer, who shall only be known as "John Doe", will be administered a dosage of drugs meant to induce death. Medical personnel will be on standby to revive John Doe at the last possible moment to bring him back from his Near-Death Experience. Dr. Peters will also be administered a dosage, but his will be lower and meant to allow him to accompany John Doe on his journey. If everything goes according to plan, then John Doe will clinically die during this procedure and Dr. Peters will be able to connect with him as they both cross over. All vitals and brain activity will be monitored and recorded during these procedures. We will begin shortly. Again, we must ask for complete silence. Thank you."

  An impressive stillness falls over the crowd as both John Doe and William are prepped. Jake waits in the wings, perspiring profusely and fidgeting. The doctor moves to John Doe's side and presses buttons on a monitored machine to begin the measured administration of the drugs. He then starts the administration of drugs to William. Both men slump on their operating tables in almost immediate sedation. The only sounds that can be heard are the various beeps and blips of the monitored equipment.

***

Nimitz looks around the room to ascertain if there are cameras, alarm systems, or anything that can alert The Council to the fact that he is no longer in his Eternity. Not seeing anything, he moves towards the door, takes a deep breath, and opens it. Much to his surprise, it opens with no problem and no alarms. He looks down the hall both ways, sees no sign of the orderlies, and steps out into the hallway.

"Alright, Benjamin," he whispers to himself, "what now? Which way do you go? If you go left, you run the risk of running into the orderlies who put you here. If you go right, you could just keep running forever. Which one is it going to be?"

He pauses for a moment, closes his eyes, and then starts walking down the hall to his right. He pauses every so often and glances through the windows into the other Eternity rooms. He is about half a mile from where he started when he comes to a T juncture. He glances down each arm. Both look the same as the hallway he is currently in. He turns to his right and looks in a few windows, seeing Eternity rooms just like his. He turns and heads down the left arm, looking in a few windows on that side. These rooms are different. They are not neutral, warm tones. They are completely black and empty. He continues down this hallway, pausing to glance in windows every so often until he reaches one window and comes to a complete stop.

Inside this room, he sees a woman hovering above the ground. Around her, though, are other people. They are misty and gray, almost ghost-like. The misty people are standing, not hovering. Nimitz watches them, trying to figure out what is happening. A few seconds goes by and then the woman disappears. A few seconds after she does, the misty people also disappear, leaving the Eternity room completely empty.

Miles into the labyrinth of hallways, it occurs to Nimitz that he has no idea where he is, where he's going, what his game plan is, nothing. He has seen more Eternity rooms and more of those black rooms with misty people in them, but he is nowhere closer to finding the woman. He stops to collect his thoughts and ends up in front of another black room where the deceased person is surrounded by misty people. He is about to start walking again when a flash of light in the upper corner of the room catches his eye. He presses his face against the glass of the window and focuses on the upper corner where the wall meets the ceiling. There is another flash of light. This time, though, there is something in the light. It takes a moment for his eyes to adjust, but Nimitz can clearly make out a man's face.

The man appears solid, in full color, as though he is alive. The man is looking at the deceased and the misty people while Nimitz is looking at the man. He looks familiar. The man looks around the room. He is on his second sweep around the room when he sees Nimitz through the window. They lock eyes. Then the man gives Nimitz a wink and a smirk before he disappears, followed by the deceased, then the misty people.

    Nimitz leans against the wall trying to decide his next move. He realizes that he doesn't know where he is and doesn't know if he will ever find Death. How would he even begin to find the woman? He is starting to wonder if it is even possible so he does what he did before: closes his eyes and takes a deep breath. After a few seconds, he opens his eyes abruptly and starts moving down the hall with new purpose.

    After a few turns and jaunts down a few more hallways, he comes to a familiar place: the outside of the utility room beneath the council room. Nimitz readies himself for a possible altercation with the orderlies since he does not know if they will be on the other side of the door. He flings open the door and takes a defensive stance. The room is empty. The chair is there and Nimitz immediately jumps into it and looks around for the way to make the chair rise back up in the council room. He sees the control panel against the back wall. He runs to the control panel, flips the switch to make the chair rise, and dashes back towards the chair. He jumps into it as it is rising through the ceiling into the council room.

Standing in the council room, Nimitz knows there is a way to move from this room back into the nothingness from whence he was pulled. He is working backwards to try to get back to Death. He looks around the room trying to remember how he had gotten into the council room before. He remembers the white dot. He remembers it growing. He remembers being in the chair facing a bald, male council member who had a white beard. He remembers that being the first face he saw when his focus came back from being in the nothingness. Nimitz realizes that means he entered from behind the chair. He looks at the back wall of the council room. He walks across the room to the wall and places his hand on it. He pushes his hand against the wall and his hand disappears through it. Nimitz steps through the wall.

Okay, Benjamin, Nimitz thinks to himself, *How do we get from here back to life? Back to Earth? Back to home. That's where I will find her. Home. I just have to get back to where we met and I will find her. How? Think, Benjamin! Think! No wait...don't think. Don't think. Just calm yourself, clear your thoughts, and you will know.*

A few seconds of silence lapses then Nimitz's figure begins to form in the black nothingness.

Nimitz looks around and realizes he is in front of his client's brownstone, where he first saw the woman. He starts walking towards his apartment. He is relishing seeing the city again, hearing the buzzing of daily activity on the streets, and just life in general.

As he gets on his street, he notices that some things look different. Little things. The store on the corner has changed names. The cars parked on the street look newer. There's an awning over the entrance of his building that wasn't there before. Nimitz approaches the entryway of his building and stops in front of the door. His brow furrowed, he slowly reaches out his hand to grip the door handle. His hand goes through the solid material. Nimitz knew he wouldn't come back to life, but the realization that he is now what would be considered a ghost or spirit stuns him briefly. He moves into the building, up the stairs, and into his old apartment. All his belongings are gone. From the interior, he surmises that he has been dead for a few years. He takes in his former surroundings and, for the first time, the fact that he died sets in and Nimitz is overcome with emotion.

"I should never have called you here. You don't belong here anymore."

Nimitz turns around, his face tear-stained, and lets out an elated sigh when he sees the woman standing behind him. He studies the woman before him, her exquisite dark skin, her black, almond-shaped eyes, and her dancer's build. She is the most beautiful woman he has ever seen. Despite never having really known her, he feels comfortable. There's a familiarity about her that calms him.

"What do you mean you never should have called me here? I came looking for you," Nimitz responds.

"I guided you. I was selfish. I wanted you to find me so I guided you. That's how you woke from your eternity. That's how you knew how to get back through to this realm."

"You wanted me to find you?" Nimitz stammers.

"I did."

Nimitz and the woman lock eyes and both blush. They do not break eye contact for a few seconds in silence.

"I know," she whispers.

"What?"

"I figured that you had millions of questions running through your head and didn't know how to make sense of any of them or how to even begin asking. I know. You can ask me anything and I will answer. You can start wherever you like."

"Is this how it happens for everyone?"

"What? Dying?"

"Yes," Nimitz sheepishly responds.

"All experiences are individual. No two are alike. Your death was yours alone."

"No. What I meant was does everyone…feel like they've fallen in love with you when they are dying?"

The woman smiles. Her whole face lights up upon hearing Nimitz say that he has fallen in love with her. "To answer that, ask yourself when you first felt like you were falling in love with me."

"I was drawn to you from the first time I saw you," Nimitz confesses. "I spent weeks trying to find you. I thought you were a member of my client's family. I didn't realize what you…who you were until I nearly died in my apartment. I think that is when I realized that I was had fallen in love with you."

"There's your answer, then. You were falling in love with me before you knew what I was. You fell in love with me before you died, so the answer to your question is no, falling in love with death is not part of dying."

"What happens now? You said I no longer belong here. Where do we go?"

"Nothing happens now. You go back to your eternity."

"No. That can't be it. Why does that have to be it?"

"You know what I am. It is impossible for us to be together."

"What if I stayed here and saw you when you came to do what it is that you do?" Nimitz half-heartedly smiles. He is fidgeting with his hands.

"In this realm, as you are now, you are what is considered a ghost or spirit," the woman explains. "The Council will allow you to remain this way if this is what you choose to do, but there are established rules by which you must abide or you will be exiled. You will still have to go back to inform The Council of your decision. It also wouldn't change the fact that we could not be together. I don't know what I was even thinking. I knew this was futile. I knew we could never be but no one has ever seen me like you do. It was special, precious. I didn't want to lose that. I was selfish. It is not fair of me to have brought you here, to have allowed you to imagine an existence with me, to let you know that I loved you only to turn you away."

"You love me?" Nimitz's voice is that of a schoolboy.

"Yes, but," the woman looks tenderly at Nimitz and her voice trails off. Nimitz starts to reach for her, but she abruptly moves away. "Don't touch me!"

Nimitz is taken aback by this and looks wounded. The woman softens her tone. "You cannot touch me. Remember what I am. You cannot touch me."

"Why not? I am already dead. What more could happen?"

"Your body died. You still exist as a soul. Your soul can also die. I exist on many levels, operate in many ways. The death of a soul is brutal, cruel. It is one of the reasons why I say that we could never be together. You could never touch me."

Nimitz takes this information in. He furrows his brow, trying to think of what to say next. He hadn't thought things through this far, so he was unsure of himself. "What is your name?"

The woman smiles, genuinely amused at his question. She has never been asked this and finds the normalcy of it almost refreshing. "I have many names from all over in thousands of languages from millions of worlds."

"What was your first name? Your birth name?"

"I was not born. I have always been. I existed before time. I only have the names that I have been given by those who have met me. Your kind calls me Death."

Nimitz feels his cheeks go flush. "I don't know what I was thinking. This is all so incredibly abstract to me. I just defaulted to the type of thing one would ask a stranger. You don't feel like a stranger, though, and it feels odd that I don't know what to call you."

"You call me Death. That is a name."

Nimitz gives her a sly smirk and then sarcastically says, "So, Death, where are you from originally?" They both laugh. Then they stare at each other for a few moments, smiling.

"You must go back, Benjamin."

"That's the first time you've said my name. Most people call me Mr. Nimitz. So much so that it almost feels like my name is Nimitz."

"I like your name. Your whole name. What would you prefer to be called?"

"I never gave it much thought, but I guess I would prefer Benjamin. My mom chose the name. There must be a reason she thought it was a good name for her only child. I guess using it would honor that."

"You must go back, Benjamin," Death repeats.

"I don't want to."

"I know."

They look away from each other. They are standing in an awkward silence like two middle school aged kids with a crush on each other. They look back to each other, staring longingly, shy smiles on their faces, knowing this is the last time they will see each other and trying to prolong it.

"Even if I wanted to go back, I have no idea how to, Nimitz finally concedes.

"The same way you got here. You just concentrate on where you want to go."

"So, this is goodbye?"

"Yes."

"I want you to know that you are the most beautiful woman I have ever seen and the only woman that I have ever fallen in love with," Nimitz breathlessly declares his love.

"I know. I would like you to know that you are the only being that I have ever encountered who has seen me this beautifully. You are the only one that has ever made me call him out from eternity."

"You are beautiful. How could you not be seen that way?"

"How I appear is chosen by the beholder, the dying. Most are afraid. To them I appear as something comforting. To others I appear as something terrifying. You saw me as something beautiful. Thank you."

"I love you."

"I love you," Death replies with emphasis on the word *you*.

Nimitz takes a deep breath, looks at her one last time, and starts to disappear. Before he fades away completely, he returns. Death looks puzzled.

"No," he says emphatically.

"What?"

"I'm not going back."

"Benjam..."

Nimitz interrupts her, "No. When I was alive, I followed all the rules. I did everything I was supposed to do: drove the speed limit, said please and thank you, ma'am and sir, never cheated on tests, left the tags on the mattresses. I was a good man, a good person. And no one cared. I had no one to share my life with. No real friends. No family. No significant other. I looked up one day and I was all alone in the world and had no idea how I had let that happen or how to change it. I don't blame anyone. I'm not mad. I just let it all go by. I colored within the lines, never stopping to see what was beyond them." Nimitz looks into Death's eyes. His eyes are wet and red. He lets out a small gasp for air and smiles. "Then I saw you. It sounds cliché, and maybe it truly is, I don't know. I've never fallen in love. I saw you and it changed me. Fundamentally. Rules and routines that I followed for years no longer mattered. I felt everything. It was as if I had just woken up from a long sleep. Every time I would see you, it would revive me. I could hear you, feel you. That's crazy, isn't it? I went crazy, didn't I? I sound like one of those men who is trying to justify why he stalked a woman. We had met once. Hadn't even met, really, just seen each other, and you were all I could think about. The next time I saw you all those feelings intensified."

Nimitz pauses, realizing he sounds manic. He looks at Death, confused and scared. He is realizing that the whole scenario sounds far-fetched and this realization is making him question everything.

"You could hear me because I spoke to you," Death says softly.

"What?"

"I spoke to you. I told you before that no one had ever seen me this beautifully. I meant that. When you saw me for the first time that day, in your client's bedroom, it did something to me. A connection was made that day. A connection that I made with you, to you, so that I could find you again. You found me again and again because I was talking to you in thoughts and dreams. We communicated for a year before I came for you."

"I won't go back. This is the most alive I have ever felt and I am not going back to my eternity to sit in some dream state forever. Not when I could be with you."

"Benjamin, you can't be with me."

"Maybe not in any traditional sense, but I can be your companion. I can be near you. I can talk with you, travel with you. I'm not going back. I'm not giving up the best thing that has ever happened to me."

"They will come for you eventually. There are rules," Death warned.

"That's fine. When they come for me, I will deal with it. For now, though, I am here with you and nothing else is of concern. I will not waste what precious time I may have with you worrying about what will happen later."

Death studied his face for a moment before smiling, "Have you ever been to Bucharest?"

Nimitz, amused by this non-sequitur, smiles broadly, "No. Why?"

"Because that is where we are going next." Death holds her hand up in front of Nimitz's face and they both instantly disappear.

***

William bolts upright on the operating table, gasping for air and clawing at the various tubes to which he is attached for monitoring. He looks around wildly, disheveled, as though he doesn't know where he is. One of the medical personnel rush to his side, attempting to calm him, and check his vitals. The doctor and remaining medical personnel are otherwise engaged at the other operating table where John Doe is coding. William hears the flatline tone from the heart monitor. He looks over to John Doe, who is non-responsive and pale. The entire room is silent save for what is happening inside the sterilized room. The audience stares on in shock, some of them silently weeping. After a few minutes, the medical personnel step away from the table and the doctor calls time of death. William stares blankly at the audience then looks off stage to Jakey, who looks back at William and shakes his head nervously.

Off stage, amid all the commotion, the director's voice can be heard. "Cut to commercial! Go to commercial, goddamnit!"

William slyly smiles at Jakey and winks.

***

Jakey is practically hyperventilating. William is laughing as he checks his cell phone for trending news of his show. He reads the headlines to Jakey with malevolent glee.

"*Show airs live death*!" William laughs. "'*Deathhunter kills someone on live TV*!' Well, technically, we didn't kill him. The doctor did." William scoffs. "*Has Deathhunter gone too far*?" William looks over to Jakey, grinning, and slaps him on the thigh playfully. Then he turns and looks out the car window. "Don't worry, Jakey. I did it. I crossed the fuck over. I did it. And I can do it again. I've got the EEG to prove it. Don't worry. We made history tonight. I made history. I'm going to change the face of death."

"Jesus Christ, William, what in the actual fuck are you going on about? We're through! The show is gonna be canceled before the goddamned sun comes up! We aired a man dying on live motherfucking television! The lawyers are gonna be up our asses! The network is gonna be up our asses! His family is gonna sue the holy living shit outta us! Oh my god, my wife is gonna fucking leave me. I'm ruined." Jakey looks like he's about to have a stroke. He's rolling the window down and breathing in the outside air deeply. William is looking at him in amusement.

"Jacob, no one is going to get sued. No one is canceling the show," William coos at him. "I did it. You don't understand. I actually crossed over tonight. I saw the afterlife. Do you know how filthy rich we are going to be? Jakey, you're going to be a millionaire."

While Jakey does not completely relax with this thought, he does manage to crack a halfhearted smile in William's direction. William just smiles at him and turns back to looking out the window.

***

There is a lot of commotion as various administrators answer phones and run from office to office. Yelling can be heard from behind a closed door that startles some of the people running about.

Are you fucking kidding me with this shit, Daniel?" An exquisitely dressed man in his early fifties shouts as he paces behind his desk. "Who in the holy hell approved this shit? How did this shit get on the air? Drug administration? Inducing death? On a live fucking television show? I want to see the goddamned contracts on this shit! Where are the goddamned contracts? Addison! Is anyone gonna fucking say anything? Addison!"

A young woman opens the office door and nervously steps in, "Sir?"

The network executive softens his tone, "Addison, sweetie, please bring me an herbal tea with honey and a goddamned Xanax. Thank you, dear." Addison exits and closes the door behind her. The network exec stands behind his desk with his back to the other people in the room. He stares out the window silently for a moment before turning back around. "Daniel," he begins again, this time more controlled, "how did this happen? Don't you have any damned control on your set?"

"We have contracts, sir. Everything was in place and had been reviewed by the

lawyers. It was all approved. I swear."
Daniel's voice is shaky.

"You're seriously telling me that you have contracts signed by all parties involved and that the network lawyers went over all of this and approved it? They approved drug administration and, basically, killing a man on live television? Is that what you're saying?"

"Yes. I swear."

"Do you have copies of these contracts?"

"With me? No. I don't."

"That's okay, Daniel. I do. Let's take a look at them, shall we? Let's look these over together. I even have one of the network lawyers that worked on them here, so this should be quick and painless." The network exec motions for the lawyer to bring over the contracts. While the lawyer is setting out the contracts, Addison returns with the tea and Xanax. She deftly maneuvers around the men and the documents to place the tea and saucer with pill on the desk and quietly exits the office, closing the door behind her.

"Percy, if you don't mind, can you review the contracts and let us know what they detail?" He sits back in his chair, pops the pill in his mouth, and then settles in, sipping his tea. He has a smug look on his face as he watches Daniel for his reaction to the contracts.

Percy quickly and quietly reviews the contracts. He then looks at the network executive with a puzzled expression on his face. "Ummm, these contracts detail what is described as being a hypnotherapy session in which Dr. Peters and a male volunteer would be hypnotized to discuss the male volunteer's recent Near-Death Experience. The desired outcome was to be that Dr. Peters would be able to somehow share the experience and cross over through hypnotherapy."

"That's not...no, those aren't the updated contracts!" Daniel explodes. "That is not what was discussed and that is not what was agreed upon. Everyone signed contracts and waivers. They talked about the drug administration and the fact that Dave, I mean John Doe, was going to be, um, you know, killed."

"Percy," the network exec's tone is one of subdued rage, "do you have the most updated contracts? Are these the correct contracts?"

"Sir, we only have one set of contracts for the show that night. Legal never would have signed off on someone being killed on live television. That was never the agreement."

"With whom were these contracts negotiated?"

Percy says, barely above a whisper, "Everything went through Daniel and Dr. Peters."

The network exec levels his eyes at Daniel and grinds his teeth. Daniel looks down at his feet for a moment, but then he snaps his head back up indignantly and slaps his open hand on the corner of the executive's desk.

"Damn it!" he exclaims.

"Excuse me?" The network exec is unmoved by the theatrics.

"I got played. *We* got played."

"How so?"

"William is the one who told me what he had worked out with the lawyers. I trusted him. I have to. He's the star of the show. Why would he jeopardize it? So, I believed him when he said that he had gotten the lawyers to agree to it all. I couldn't believe it at first, but he explained how he was able to convince you all that this would make scientific, television, and human history and that you all agreed to let him do it. So, I signed the goddamned contracts without looking them over again. I trusted him."

The office door opens and William and Jakey walk in. Jakey looks mousy and twitchy, like he's about to be the cat's dinner. William, alternately, looks like he is about the make the deal of a lifetime.

"Gentlemen, thank you for joining us. You're late."

"Of course, I tried to get here as soon as I could, but I don't know if you heard or not, I briefly died yesterday and it took a little time to wake up this morning," William smiles broadly at the room to no amusement.

"Of course, I heard. That's why we are here. According to my lawyer and your director, the contracts that we have are not the contracts that you advertised. Care to explain that?"

"Nope. Why waste time with inconsequential things?"

"I'm sorry. Inconsequential?" The executive is used to the grandeur and ego of entertainers, but he is nonplussed at William's shake off.

"You're worried that your network will get sued. It won't. You're worried that you'll get fired. You won't. So, yeah, these things are inconsequential. We're wasting time."

"Did you come back from the dead with psychic abilities? Is that how you have knowledge of things that have yet to happen…or not happen?"

"No, but I did come back from the dead. I know what I know because I know that money is all that matters and, Paul, I'm about to make you and this network a shit ton of money." William leans across the network executive's desk and smiles.

"How do you figure?"

"Have you even looked online? The show was a fucking hit! Death is a draw these days, gentlemen. People film it with their phones. Killers post their murders online. Seeing it in a medical setting online is nothing. Like it was scripted. Nobody gave a shit that Dave died."

"For chrissakes, William!" Jacob blurts. "Have some damned decency. And quit using his real fucking name!"

"Oh, forgive me! I apparently haven't properly mourned the man who basically agreed to be killed on television so he could get paid. Oh, poor John Doe. He was a fucking wastoid. By the way, he had no known living family. You're welcome, Paul. There's a reason why he was chosen. The more relevant point is that I accomplished what I meant to accomplish. I crossed over last night. People don't care about Dave dying. What they're posting about this morning is what happened. Did I succeed? Do I have proof of life after death? They want answers. They want to know what happened. I've been on the phone all morning with people who want to fund my next attempt. I've been reading comments from people saying they want to be the next volunteer. I even had a representative from Madison Fucking

Square Garden call to ask if I would want to host the next live show there."

William pauses for a moment. All eyes are on him. The others in the room are silent and listening intently to him. He stands before the window, surveying the skyline before him studiously, concentrating on his next words. He turns to face them with a serious face and tone. "Gentlemen, contracts mean nothing now. We've got to move forward and give the people what they want. I need to start planning the next attempt. I need more time and practice, but I believe I can capture death."

***

Nimitz walks around a living room looking at items belonging to the owner. Death is in another room. There is a man sitting on the couch watching television.

Nimitz wanders over to the window and glances out. He stares at a billboard on one of the buildings across the street. It has a picture of a man with the word DEATHHUNTER emblazoned diagonally across the board like in vintage circus ads.

A flash of recognition crosses Nimitz's face.

Death comes out of the room and approaches Nimitz. As she holds her hand up in front of Nimitz's face, he hears a woman scream from the other room.

"She won't wake up! Tony! The baby won't wake up!"

The man on the couch runs towards the nursery and passes through fading images of Death and Nimitz as they disappear.

Nimitz looks again at the billboard. He remembers the man in the eternity room with the misty people.

"How do near death experiences work?" he asks.

"What do you mean?"

"I've heard stories my whole life about people claiming to have died and returned, people seeing white lights and deceased family members, going to heaven before being sent back. Is that all just a dream, hallucination, or drug-induced fantasy? Or is it real?"

"It is real."

"When I got out of my eternity room, I was wandering through some hallways trying to find my way out. I saw these black rooms. In more than one of them, I saw the deceased surrounded by some people that seemed to be made from mist. The deceased would stay for a little while, a few minutes maybe, then disappear. Then the misty people would disappear. Is that where it happens? I mean, is that, if you don't fully die, where you go? Briefly?"

"In a near death experience, I am summoned, but not as harvester, so to speak. A near death experience causes enough trauma to the body and mind that dying is a possibility, but not necessarily a definite. The soul is taken to eternity to be protected while decisions are made. If I am needed further, then I harvest the soul. If I am not, then the soul is transported back into the body. Much like any eternity, each is different. Some experience a warm feeling as they approach what they believe to be heaven. Others see loved ones. Still others see dark hallways, tunnels, or themselves. What you witnessed was a near death experience, yes."

"Can the living appear in someone else's near death experience?"

"I'm not sure I understand."

"The one that I witnessed. There was someone else there. He wasn't in the room exactly, but he was there. The deceased was hovering, the misty people were standing around, and then up in the corner of the room, where the wall meets the ceiling, I saw another person. A man. That man." Nimitz points to the billboard, indicating the man in the picture. Death looks to the billboard then back at Nimitz. "He was looking down into the eternity room. It was like someone lifting a lid to peek in a box. He was completely fleshed out, fully colored, solid, and illuminated like it was daytime where he was. He saw me. He was looking around the room. I was in the hallway peering through the window in the door and he saw me. He smirked at me, winked, and then disappeared."

Death looks at Nimitz steadily, seriously. Then she looks to the billboard again before furrowing her brow.

Nimitz sighs heavily and says, "That's not supposed to happen, is it?"

"No. The only way the living enter eternity is either through dying or a near death experience. To have one enter on his or her own while still alive is most certainly not supposed to happen."

Death puts her hand in front of Nimitz's face and they disappear.

***

William and Paul are standing backstage on the set of Deathhunter.

"This is it!" William exclaims as he gestures to the setup on the stage. "This is the way to go! It's all ready!" Paul looks dubious and William picks up on this. "I'm going to do it all. No volunteers. I'm the one that's going under, so you don't have to worry about any lawsuits. I know you are always worried about the lawsuits."

"That doesn't make it any better, Will. You know that. You're the talent. If something fucks up, and you bite it on air, we lose the talent, the show, the merchandising, all of it. Volunteer, no volunteer, either way, we're fucked."

"Wow, Paul, thanks. Your concern over possibly losing me is touching, really."

"Fuck you, Will. You've been a pain in my ass for years now. I'm just being straight with you. I am not behind this. I think this is lunacy and I want it shut the fuck down, but I also know numbers and you are rocking the fucking numbers, so I am stuck here. You know the show is going to go on. You know this. Advertisers are throwing money at us to sponsor your shows. People are willing to pay out the ass for tickets to see you. We can't make the merch fast enough to keep the orders filled. You know the show is happening, so quit trying to grease me up."

"This is different, Paul. I've been doing a lot of research. I know what I am doing here. I'm using myself not only to save the network the hassle of the possible lawsuits. I'm using myself because I know what I'm doing. Trust me. We're making history here…and, if I succeed, we could just fucking change life as we know it." William slaps his hand onto Paul's shoulder and looks him solidly in the eyes. He smiles and winks at Paul.

The room goes black. The audience is silent. A single low spotlight comes up on the stage. William stands in the spotlight, solemn and still. A moment passes in silence with him standing there.

"Tonight, ladies and gentlemen, fellow travelers, skeptics, and believers," he opens, "we once again step into the breach together. I have spent the last two decades or so of my life attempting to discover what lies beyond this life. I have tried to solve the mystery of what happens after we die. As many of you know, we have once attempted to do what we are doing here tonight. That attempt, though it provided some success, ended in tragedy with the death of our volunteer, our friend, Dave. While I stand by my research, theories, and methods, the death of my friend at the hand of my pursuit has weighed heavily on me. That's why, tonight, there will be no volunteers. Tonight, I will be the one who will be put under. I will be the one crossing over." There are audible murmurs and gasps from the audience. "Please, ladies and gentlemen, please don't be concerned. I have an excellent medical team, I am in good health, and I have researched and learned more since our last journey. I am confident that, tonight, I will make contact and return to you safely. To say that I am not nervous would be a lie. I've never lied to you, dear believers, and I will not begin tonight. I am nervous. I do want to say, before we begin, that if anything should happen, thank you for believing in me, supporting me, helping me, encouraging me, and accompanying me through all of this. If I don't return, know that I made it across. Even if I don't make it back. I thank you for everything. Please join me now as we cross over and hunt Death!"

There is thunderous applause as the audience cheers. Many are crying. Others appear worried. William crosses the stage as the lights come up to reveal a sterilized medical room much like in the first attempt. The only difference is that there is only one operating table. William props himself up onto the table, looks out into the audience, smiles, winks, and gives a wave. The audience cheers again.

William lays back onto the table and the medical personnel start attaching monitors to him. The doctor comes over and oversees the administration of drugs. The room is silent except for the sound of the machines. Within a short period of time, William appears to be sleeping. The monitors register a standard heart rate and brain activity. A few moments pass and the monitors start beeping erratically. A woman in the audience screams. This causes a disturbance in the audience. Murmuring, uneasiness, and a few gasps escape the crowd.

William sits up straight on the operating table, startling the doctor and medical personnel. He still appears to be under the influence of the drug, but his eyes are now open. He turns his head and looks into the wings of the stage. He lifts his arm and points offstage. He gets off the table as the doctor and medical personnel rush over to stop him. Before they can, a loud noise is heard off stage from the direction in which William is pointing. Audience members scream and gasp as Jakey collapses in the wings and the top portion of his body can be seen from behind the curtains.

As the doctor and medical personnel rush over to Jakey, William also crosses the stage. The cameras continue to follow the action, with one cameraman following William specifically. William approaches Jakey, who is gasping and clutching his heart. William kneels beside Jakey. The camera pulls in close on them both. Jakey is looking up at William. He looks scared. He grabs at William's arm.

William calmly says, "Tell me what you see."

Gasping and struggling for words, Jakey manages to get out, "Dog. Black dog."

"The black dog. Is it sitting to your right? Across from me?" William asks, his eyes intensely focused on what appears to be empty space across from him. Jakey nods rapidly. He is trying to pull himself closer to William. "The black dog is licking your hand. Am I right?"

"Yes. Is it going to bite me?"

"Nooo," William says soothingly. "I don't think it is a dog."

William is staring directly at Death, who is knelt on Jakey's right, his hand held to her lips. Nimitz is standing behind her. To William and Jakey, she appears as a black dog. To Nimitz, she is still the beautiful woman he has known her to be. Death is focused on Jakey. William is looking at Death. Jakey is looking from Death to William.

In a rush of adrenaline, Jakey manages to compose himself enough to spit out, "You see it, don't you? You see it? You see Death! You son of a bitch! You did it, didn't you? You did it."

The doctor and medical personnel push William to the side, but he does not break his focus on Death. The doctor and medical personnel work to stabilize Jakey. They lift him and bring him over to the operating table. The cameras follow the action except for the one cameraman who stays focused on William. For a moment, Death and William make eye contact. Then Death moves over to Jakey's side. William watches Death walk away and notices Nimitz. They stare at each other: Nimitz sternly, William confused. Nimitz steps away to move closer to Death. William collapses on the floor, still looking in Nimitz's direction, with a smile on his face.

"He's gone. We lost him."

***

Death and Nimitz are standing outside of a barn. The body of a young man can be seen lying on the ground inside the barn behind them. Death is raising her hand to Nimitz's face when he stops her.

"Wait. He saw you, you know?"

"They all see me, Benjamin."

"No. Not him." Nimitz glances over his shoulder to the body in the barn. He looks at him for a moment, considering his words. "I meant the guy on the show. The host. He saw you."

"Yes, I know. He saw you as well."

"He wasn't the one who was dying, though. And he saw you."

"You weren't dying when you first saw me. You were just open to it. So was he. He was looking for me. I just happened to appear while he was in an open state. Much like you."

"I understand that, but I wasn't looking for you when I first saw you."

"No, but you were open. You were experiencing something in your life that opened you up to the possibilities outside. You were searching for something. Does that make sense?"

"Yes, it does. Why did he see you in the same way as the dying man? I thought you appeared in the manner designated by the dying. Would two people see you the same way?"

"I am sure that I have appeared in the same form more than once. The incident is interesting, though, because it is rare that multiple people see me in the same form at the same time. He was under the influence of the drugs, though. That could account for it."

"I'm confused. How would you appear differently to more than one person at one time?"

"My darling, at any given time, there are multiple people dying all over simultaneously. I am not bound by the same laws as you or any other creature. As I am standing here talking to you, I am also in thousands of other places as well."

Nimitz stares at her blankly for a moment, trying to grasp the full meaning of her words. He looks up to the early morning sky and the few remaining stars. "You are here and everywhere all at once," he says in amazement.

"Yes."

"And you are a thousand different things to a thousand different people all at once."

"Yes."

"And it doesn't concern you that a man calling himself 'Deathhunter' was able to see you?"

"What concerns me is what you creatures do to yourselves and each other. Sadly, even that only concerns me a little as this is what I am. There are many that can see me, sense me, and feel me."

"Yes, but he wants to capture you. Maybe even kill you."

"I am not something that can be captured or killed."

"Are you sure of that?"

"I existed long before your kind. I have been hunted by many, capture by none." Death looks at Nimitz, smiles coyly, lifts one eyebrow, and then winks at him. This makes Nimitz blush and he smiles back, broadly. She raises her hand and they disappear.

***

"I'm in love with him." The statement is bold, yet gentle. "Did you know that?" Ferrol asks Heather through tears.

"I did, sweetie. I think we all knew." Heather softly responds, cradling her friend's head.

"It's so stupid. I know Ben isn't gay. I mean, I had hope that maybe he was repressed, closeted. I know what that's like. Growing up a black, gay man in small town, Southern Louisiana, I knew that most people I would encounter would not be all too open to that. Even New Orleans back then wasn't completely open. The lights in the French Quarter still go dark right before you get to the gay clubs. So, even though Ben never said outright whether he was gay or straight, I always thought maybe he was. Then he announced that he had met a woman and I lost all hope. Don't misunderstand, I was happy for him, but it still stung."

"I know it did. And honestly, I think we all kinda thought the same thing and were hoping that you two would end up together," Heather admits.

"Is...Do you all think Ben is gay?"

"It doesn't matter right now, Ferrol," Hayden sighs. "Just know that we were in your court. Both of yours."

"So stupid," Ferrol weakly throws his hands up in the air. "The whole thing is just so stupid. I'm over here wondering if he's gay, if he even supports interracial relationships, if he could possibly be into me, and poor Ben is..." His voice trails off as he sits down and stares at the ground.

"Well, I can at least answer one of those questions for you," Hayden offers. "He supports interracial relationships."

"Yeah? Well at least that's something."

"Yeah, when we were in law school, we were both groomsmen at our friends' wedding. We went to college with Kisu and Beth. Kisu is black. Beth is white. Ben stood up at their wedding and was so happy for them. Even gave a great toast. So, yeah, he supports interracial relationships. So if he is gay and into you, you being black wouldn't be an issue for him."

"This entire conversation is moot now. I'm sorry. I just felt the need to confess, I guess."

"It's no problem, man," Dean says. "I think we are all on the same page right about now."

"He had a premonition he was going to die," Ferrol announces, his voice shaking. "And I told him it was nothing."

"Wait, what? When did he say that?" Jeanne asks incredulously. "That doesn't sound like Benji."

"We had coffee one afternoon a few months ago. He said there was something he wanted to talk to me about. He confided in me that he believed that he had seen death on multiple occasions. He said that death was a woman and that he had seen her more than once, that he had fallen in love with her, and that he believed that he was going to die soon."

"Holy..." Hayden puts his head in his hands, defeated.

"That just doesn't sound like Benji." Jeanne repeats.

"What did you tell him?" Heather asks.

"I told him that he is in proximity to death quite a bit in his profession and that, given his last client actually passed away with him in the room and he has yet to allow himself to truly grieve the loss of both of his parents, his subconscious is acting out and manifesting this death as a woman delusion as a means of processing the grief and turning it into something beautiful."

"Wow," Dean exhales. "That is deep. I can see why you earn the big bucks, man."

"It's beautiful," Heather responds.

"But I basically blew off his premonition," laments Ferrol. "I mean, in all of that there was evidence of a true fear and I ignored it. I can't help but wonder if I let my personal emotions get the better of me."

"I don't think you did. I think you nailed it. I've thought about it for a while now and I know, we all know, that Nim never dealt with Asher's and Lida's deaths. I don't know what made him think he was going to die. I don't know how all that shit works...how mothers can lift overturned cars in the heat of the moment to rescue their babies, how some people call right when you're thinking of them, how twins separated at birth find each other in their thirties and realize that they drive the same car, both married women named Mary, and both named their kids Donna and Jack. I don't understand any of it, but I understand what you told him and it makes sense to me," Hayden pats Ferrol lightly on the shoulder.

"Either way, here we are," Ferrol sighs heavily. "I love him, you know?" Ferrol gets up and excuses himself to the restroom to wash his face and compose himself. Dean walks down the hall to make a phone call, leaving Heather, Jeanne, and Hayden in the room.

"You...you both know, don't you? Or at least suspect? Right? I can't be the only one." Hayden hesitantly broaches the subject with the two women.

"I've suspected for decades," Heather says. "It's why I gave you that look when he announced that he had met someone and talked about a woman that night at dinner. Benji's never come out and said he was gay, but I've thought it since about junior high."

"Maybe he's bi," Jeanne offers. "I wasn't expecting the mystery someone to be a woman either, but let's be honest here. It's not like Benji's an open book."

"He didn't want to disappoint them." Hayden announces sadly.

"What?" Heather and Jeanne both respond in unison.

"Asher and Lida. In college, there was this one time where I think he got caught off guard by a guy at a party. The guy made a move and I could tell by Nim's reaction that he was both excited and repelled by it. I could also tell that the subsequent discussion that he had with me about it made him nervous. I told him that the guy was drunk and didn't know what he was doing. I shrugged it off as nothing more than a party foul, so that Nim wouldn't feel uncomfortable. Then I made sure to make it known that being gay was no big deal to me. I wanted him to know that, if he were gay, it wouldn't end our friendship. That I was cool with it. I just knew I couldn't say it that way. He relaxed when I said it, but there was something in the way he talked about the guy...he said something about how did the guy ever tell his parents and what if he were an only child, how that could destroy their hopes for him. That wasn't about the guy at the party. I mean, it was, but he was projecting. I knew that night that Nim was gay. So yeah, maybe bisexual. Shit, none of it makes sense, though. Death? Death is a woman and Nimitz is in love with her? Come on! That makes no sense."

"Unless he couldn't come to terms with it because he is so afraid of breaking his parent's hearts." Jeanne said sadly.

"Asher and Lida loved Benji so much. He never could have broken their hearts. He has to know that. It bothers me to think that he doesn't know that. They would have loved him no matter who he chose to love."

The three friends sat in silence as the sun set in the world outside.

***

"I don't understand this, Paul. It was a success! Again! This makes the second show that I've done with this method and the second success. And you're telling me that you're pulling the plug? Shutting it down? Why in the hell are you doing that? The advertisers were-"

"The advertisers immediately pulled out once Jakey died on air. Yes, the show pulls in the views. Yes, the show pulls in the money and gets asses in the seats. Will, you've done it twice…and two men have died. Ratings don't fucking matter in the public opinion of morality. We can't keep doing this, Will. Next time it could be you dying. Don't you even think about that? Do you even give a shit about Jakey dying?"

"Don't you ever fucking talk to me about Jake! Jake was with me for twenty fucking years. I haven't slept since Jakey died, but I also know Jakey was behind me on this. Jakey supported the whole damned thing. Shit yeah, he was nervous about the fucking lawsuits or me losing my damned job. He always sweated the legal shit. He always worried about it going down in flames. That's who he was and that was his fucking job! Just like it is my job to do the research, put it on the line, and come out with the people in the palm of my hand. And I've done that for you. For years. And now, when I'm so fucking close I can actually see it – I fucking saw death, Paul. I fucking saw death sitting next to Jakey, like a dog, licking his hand. You know I saw it. Jakey said it. On camera. On my show. On your network. That's fucking history, man! Decades from now, people will still be talking about that. Don't do this, Paul. I'm begging you. Don't."

"It's done, Will. It's out of my hands. I can't stop it. I'm sorry. The show is canceled, effective immediately. I'm sorry, Will."

"It's a mistake."

Paul walks around to the front of his desk and sits on the corner of it in front of William. He leans in and puts his hand on William's shoulder. "Take some time, Will. The show netted you a dime or two. Go somewhere. Clear your head. Decide what you want to do next. You're a great entertainer. Give it a little bit and come back to me and we can discuss new avenues for your talents."

William, defeated, whispers, "Go somewhere."

"Yeah. Take some time. I think it will do you some good."

"You know what, Paul? I think you're right." William stands up, shakes Paul's hand, and turns to walk out of the office, whispering to himself as he exits, "You're so right."

CHAPTER THREE

William is sitting at a table in front of a pile of books. He is completely engulfed in one particularly large, ancient book. He is making notes in a battered notebook as he reads. He is weathered and tired, but intensely focused. A woman enters the reading room causing William to look up as though he has been startled awake. He immediately jumps to his feet and extends his hands out to the woman.

"Dr. Wagdy, thank you so much for coming. I know I have probably been a bother to you and I apologize."

Dr. Wagdy shakes William's hand and then takes a seat at the table opposite him. "Please, call me Nawal, and you have been no bother. It is not that often that I get a Westerner interested in Kemetism. Of course, I was intrigued."

"I am grateful that you've taken the time to meet with me."

"If I may ask, what led you to me?"

"I have been doing research on death for many years. In recent months, my research has led me to ancient Egyptian practices. I wasn't interested in the glorified movie versions of the history. I wanted something more in depth, more recent. That's how I found Kemetism. I wanted to find someone that could possibly educate me on it. I found your name as part of my research. I know this is presumptuous of me, but I'm afraid I don't have the time to audit one of your courses."

"I do research, too, Dr. Peters. I don't make a habit of meeting strange, American men in private reading rooms. I know who you are. Your credentials, well, they were impressive."

"I take it you didn't like my show?"

"I am not here to pass any kind of judgment on you. I just don't understand how someone with your academic and professional backgrounds ends up the ringleader of a circus side show. Harvard. Johns Hopkins Medical School. A successful private practice. What led you from that to hosting a show where you hunt ghosts and spirits?"

"Sometimes we can't outrun our demons. Did you come to the side show to gawk at the freak or are you here to help me with my research?"

"I want to be clear on the nature of your research. I get that you are fascinated by death to the point of obsession, but what answer are you looking for exactly?"

"I want to know how to capture death."

Dr. Wagdy laughs incredulously. "If that were possible, don't you think civilizations before ours would have already done it? What you are proposing is fantasy. Death is an inevitable, unstoppable part of life."

"I disagree. I think many cultures, ancient and modern, have stumbled upon ways to capture death. I think the problem they faced is the Tower of Babel."

Intrigued, Dr. Wagdy asks, "How do you mean?"

"I believe they each had pieces to the puzzle, but were unable to put the entire thing together because they didn't, or couldn't, communicate with each other. We are talking civilizations, cultures, and peoples across history. None of them succeeded because they only had pieces. Put all the pieces together and, I believe, it creates one master ritual to capture and conquer death."

"You are talking magic. Magic and fantasy. This is pure smoke. What information do you want from me?"

William leans in across the table closer to Dr. Wagdy and whispers, "I am looking for the complete Coffin Texts and The Book of Two Ways."

Dr. Wagdy laughs again. "You speak of them as though they are blessed or cursed, whispers amongst sarcophagi and mummies. There are digital versions of them available on the website for this very library."

"Those are not the complete texts. Don't condescend to me. You, yourself, just praised my academic and professional background. I'm not a simpleton. Where can I find the complete texts?"

Dr. Wagdy shifts uncomfortably in her seat. "I cannot speak with authority, but I have heard that there is a place that specializes in dark objects, relics of the past. It is in the marketplace in Cairo. The front is an incense shop. The keeper of the store is a man named Farouk. He might be able to help you more than I."

"Thank you, Dr. Wagdy. I am sorry I wasted your time."

"It was no waste. If nothing else, it will make for an interesting story at faculty parties. Dr. Peters, I wish you well in your research and in your pursuits. Please do not misunderstand my incredulity for flippancy. Egyptians have had a long relationship with death. I respect it as if it were a breathing entity. I do not believe it is able to be captured as would a real breathing entity, though. Ours has always been a history of preparing for death and what happens after it. I guess I just cannot imagine a world without it. Good luck in your endeavors and please take care."

Dr. Wagdy shakes hands with William and then exits the reading room. William takes a slow, deep breath, holds it for a moment, and then exhales. He then starts packing the pile of books into his satchel. He grabs his notebook and heads out of the library.

***

William is slowly making his way through the marketplace, looking at each shop, stall, and kiosk for the one described by Dr. Wagdy. He has been into three shops with incense, but has yet to find a man named Farouk. Towards the end of the marketplace, he stops to ask one of the shopkeepers if there is another marketplace in the heart of Cairo when he notices a man across the walk lifting the corner of a hanging carpet like a curtain and disappearing behind it. He notices, while the carpet is lifted, the distinct cylinder containers of colored sticks coupled with brass and wooden burners and holders. He excuses himself and darts across the walk. He hesitates for a second, aware that he is a foreigner in this land, before he lifts the corner of the carpet and steps into the incense shop. The air in the small stall is pungent and thick, smoke wafting in thin streams from a few burning incense sticks. Two men stare at him from the back of the stall. Fumbling with a translation book, William realizes that it never occurred to him that Farouk might not speak English.

"I am to look Farouk. I to come here by Dr. Nawal Wagdy." William can tell by the looks on the men's faces that his Arabic is less than perfect.

"I am Farouk." the man behind the counter says in almost pristine English. "I do not know anyone by the name Nawal Wagdy. Who really sent you?"

"Dr. Wagdy sent me, although she admitted that she has never been here or met you. She only knew of rumors of you and that you might be able to assist me."

"Why would I want to assist a stranger sent by another stranger informed only by rumors?" The second man scoffs at this remark.

"I seek the complete Coffin Texts and The Book of Two Ways."

Both Farouk and the second man get very serious looks on their faces. Farouk ushers William to join them at the back of the stall. "These texts are not forbidden or taboo. They are just seen as the remnants of a past that most modern Egyptians no longer place much faith in. The only reason they have been relegated to backroom exchanges is because, even though people no longer practice these beliefs, they still hold much reverence and fear. There are edited copies that can be accessed, purchased, or viewed at museums and libraries. The complete versions are the ones that you will find in places such as this."

"So, you have them? Both of them?"

"Yes. Give me one moment." Farouk disappears into the back of the stall, leaving William with the second man. He is staring hard at William, making him uncomfortable. William walks around the small stall, pretending to look at the wares as a means to escape the intense glare of the second man.

"Deathhunter!" The man calls out with a thick accent. William spins around to face him. The man is pointing at William and grinning. "Deathhunter! I see your show online. Big fan. My apologies for Dave and Jakey."

"Thank you."

Farouk returns from the back room with two books. The second man excitedly speaks to him in Arabic, pointing at William. "Ahhh, Mahmoud has told me who you are. I must confess I am not as familiar with your show as he is, but I do know of your work. Now we know why you seek these texts. You are looking for the portions that have been edited out. Will these be used for your next journey?"

"They quite possibly could assist, yes."

"Here you are then. No charge."

"No, I insist on paying."

"I will not accept. As a seeker of knowledge, a practicing Kemetic, and one who believes that we do not know everything, I offer these texts as gifts for your journey."

"Thank you. Thank you both. I appreciate your encouragement and generosity. Thank you." William exits the stall, steps back into the loud marketplace, and starts to head back to his hotel. He walks back the way he came, maneuvering through the crowds of tourists and shopkeepers. Up ahead of him, he notices a crowd gathering in front of one of the shops. There is a lot of excited utterances in Arabic. He moves to the side of the walk to avoid the crowd, but something catches his eye that makes him stop suddenly.

Death is kneeling next to an elderly woman. Nimitz is standing behind Death, looking over her shoulder with concern.

Death is speaking to the woman in Arabic. The woman is looking at Death who appears to her as sleek grey cat. William looks to the woman, then to Death, then to Nimitz.

Nimitz looks up suddenly, feeling eyes on him. He scans the crowd and sees a man staring at him. Nimitz recognizes William. They lock eyes. William smirks at Nimitz and then casts his eyes downward towards Death. He then looks back up to Nimitz. William points to Death and then makes a motion with his finger across his throat like he is slashing his throat. William smirks as Nimitz's eyes grow wide with fear and anger. William turns to leave the scene and Nimitz is about to give chase when something snaps his attention back to the scene before him. The woman has inexplicably started speaking in English. The accent is thick, but it is definitely English.

"I'm in love with him. Did you know that? I did, sweetie. I think we all knew."

Nimitz leans in to try to hear her more clearly, but it's too late. She is gone and Death is looking at Nimitz, perplexed.

"What is it?"

"Did she speak in English? I heard her speaking English. Did you hear it?"

"Benjamin, she spoke Arabic, not English."

"No, I heard her speaking English. She said something about being in love with a guy and asked if you knew that. Then she answered for you and said that she did, that they all knew. Is that normal? I haven't experienced that with you yet, with someone dying, deathbed confessional things. I've heard about them, but I didn't know people would just spontaneously speak in another language."

"Benjamin, look at me." Nimitz met her gaze quietly. "She spoke only Arabic. She did not say the things you heard her say. Why are you so agitated?"

Her questions reminds Nimitz. "He was here. He was right here. He was looking right at us."

"Who was here?"

"The Deathhunter."

Death puts her hand in front of Nimitz's face and instantly they are transported to the side of a road flanked by quiet, dark fields. There is a car crunched into a tree by the side of the road at a bend. A dark silhouette can be discerned hunched against the steering wheel. Death walks towards the car.

"There were no drugs this time."

"What?"

"He saw us again, but there were no drugs this time. He wasn't hooked up to any machines."

Death stands next to the window of the car; her hand is smoothing the hair of the hunched man. She appears to him in all white, illuminated in the dark. She looks over to Nimitz and says, "I do not have to tell you that the absence of machines does not equal the absence of drugs, but I do understand your meaning. Again, some are able to see me and you as well in your new state. They are just open to it. Considering we were just in an ancient city in which I play a huge part of their ancient belief system, it would not surprise me to find that many in that marketplace could see me. And you." She looks consolingly at the man and coos, "It's time to leave now. It is okay to let go."

Death can see the concern and fear on Nimitz's face. She can tell this is bothering him and that her lack of concern is not helping. "Benjamin, I know you are worried. I know you feel that I am in danger, but I promise you, I am not. You are new to my world. You see things with fresh eyes that I have been familiar with for eons. I understand that some of these things can be alarming, disconcerting, confusing, or terrifying to you. You need to understand and accept, though, that I know and understand these things. I am safe. I am protected."

"Okay. I've never been in this position. I have never been in a situation in which I feel that someone I love is in danger. Seeing that man and knowing his intentions against you just brings out some sort of primal force. I am compelled to protect you from him."

"I appreciate the instinct."

"I will try to control it."

Death turns away from the car and steps incredibly close to Nimitz. Her black eyes reflect the moon as she looks at him. They remain this way for a moment before she places her hand in front of his face.

***

William is sitting at a table in front of a computer. He is recording a video. There is a single lamp on the table next to him to provide some light. Other than that, the warehouse is dark. William is disheveled. He hasn't shaved and his hair is a little overgrown.

William addresses the video camera, "I believe that I have put it all together. I believe that I now have the knowledge needed to complete my journey. I no longer have a team to assist me and I am no longer supported by a network. This won't deter me from continuing my research and my experiments. I just need to figure out a different way to manage it. There will need to be some more research before I make another attempt. I will not give up…not when I am so close. That's all I have for now. Thanks for supporting me, believers. Goodnight."

He posts the video and moves to another area of the warehouse where there is a large bulletin board. Next to it, there is another table filled with books and papers.

The bulletin board has multiple pictures, pages copied from books, and handwritten notes pinned to it. William turns on another lamp on this table and sits down at the table. He surveys his research. He does this regularly. He stares at the bulletin board and leans back in his chair, whispering to himself, "Where will you go next? Where can I catch up to you?" He scans the postings on the board before his eyes stop on a picture copied from a text on Zoroastrianism in India. His eyes light up. The picture depicts the spirit of a human hovering over the human's remains with family members mourning the death. He runs his finger over the picture. "Three days. They hang around for three days. That's how I catch up to you."

William gets up from the table and takes out his cell. He dials a number and waits for an answer.

"George, it's Will Peters. I need you to find me a short-term rental in Little India. Smack in the center. Cost doesn't matter. Might need a six month. Details don't matter. As long as it has electric and Wi-Fi. Studio, one bedroom, fifteen bedrooms, I don't give a shit. I need it ASAP. Call me as soon as you've got something tomorrow."

He looks back at the bulletin board and smiles then turns out the lights.

***

Death and Nimitz are standing quietly on the rocky shore. Death is about to raise her hand to Nimitz's face when he speaks, "Do you have memories?"

"Yes."

"What is your first memory?"

"I don't know. I don't believe my memory works like yours. For me it is more sensory. I remember how souls feel."

"Well then, the first soul that you remember: What did it feel like?"

Death pauses for a moment, staring up to the night sky, and thinking. "The first feeling I remember is warmth."

"What other feelings do you get from souls?"

"Peace. Love. Fear. Sacrifice. Sadness. Loneliness. Happiness. Surrender. Hate. There are so many feelings. They're like stars…millions of them, seemingly close, yet I cannot really touch them."

Nimitz can see the glint of tears in Death's eyes. He fumbles with his words. He has something he wants to ask her, but is having difficulty figuring out how to ask it. "I know that you've said that you love me, but I just, I mean, I don't know how to ask this…Do you have feelings? Oh, I hope that doesn't offend you. It's just that, right here in this moment, I just realized that you are death. The Death. The Grim Reaper. The Harvester of Souls. I mean, I knew that before, but it was abstract. Now, it is real and I am confused about how you could love me if you're not a person." Nimitz looks up to see Death staring at him in a blank manner. He feels the heat rise in his cheeks as his embarrassment becomes apparent. He has put his foot in his mouth. "I am so sorry…"

"No. You don't have anything that you need to apologize for. It is a logical question. This was not a scenario that could be imagined as neither of us had ever been in an analogous situation. Now that we're here, it only makes sense that questions will arise."

"Thank you for understanding. It changes nothing. I still love you and want to be with you. It was just a thought that popped into my head."

"While you are correct in your assessment that I am not a person, I am, however, a collection of the feelings of all the souls that I have harvested. I have taken in pieces of every soul, tokens, and they have added to my being. One cannot experience souls on such an intimate level as I do without being touched, scarred, or shaped by them. I know love. I also know peace, fear, sacrifice, sadness, loneliness, happiness, surrender, and hate. I have been touched by these feelings and so many more. I know love, Benjamin. I have felt it touch me before, just never so strongly as when I met you."

"I'm sorry if I upset you with my question."

"You didn't upset me. You made me understand why your kind has these emotions. You only have so much time and you experience so much and so little in the time you have that you carry it all within you. It is simultaneously beautiful and tragic. It can be overwhelming."

"Yes, it can. Even more so when you realize you come in contact with these emotions at the exact moment when my kind is becoming fully aware that it is all over, that there is no more time. I cannot imagine the fierce rush of emotion that must overcome you in that moment as well."

Death repeats in a whisper, "It can be overwhelming." She raises her hand to Nimitz's face.

***

William walks out of a Zoroastrian Center with a few other individuals who are mostly of Indian descent. They stop together on the sidewalk, talking. Then the group separates as some of the others walk to their respective homes or next destinations. William and two of the men are left together. They continue to walk and talk as they head down the street.

"I'm very excited at the opportunity to discuss this with you further, Dr. Nimmagadda," William says to the older of the two Indian gentlemen.

"Please, call me Sekhar. I am glad to find you are interested in Zoroastrianism. It does not have a wide following in the Western world as we have learned living here."

"Thank you, Sekhar. I don't know how much Rama has told you about my research and what I hope to glean from it."

"Not much. I know that you are primarily interested in the beliefs on death and afterlife. Is this correct?"

"Yes."

They approach a small café with tables out front. "Gentlemen," Rama, the younger of the two Indian men addresses them, "why don't we take a seat here? We can discuss all the mysteries of the universe over a nice cup of tea. Will, I believe it would be best to have you explain to the good doctor what you are researching. That is, of course, unless you both have prior commitments elsewhere?"

"I'm free," offers William.

"Excellent idea," Sekhar agrees. They take seats at one of the outdoor tables. A waiter comes over to take their orders.

"Darjeeling, please."

"I would like ronga sah, please."

"Thank you, I will take a masala chai."

"Also, a tray of biscuits, please." The waiter disappears back into the restaurant. "No reason why we cannot enjoy a little sweet during such a heady conversation as we most certainly will have," Rama explains with a smile.

"Well," opens William, "where would you like me to begin?"

Sekhar wryly answers, "I always find the beginning to be a good place to begin."

"Right. I am a licensed psychiatrist. I spent most of my professional career working with patients in a psychotherapy setting. Normally psychotherapy is handled by psychologists, social workers, or licensed counselors, but I preferred to be hands on with my patients. After a few years, I turned the focus of my practice to those dealing with traumatic grief experienced from the loss of a loved one. I spent time working with a patient who had a near death experience and was suffering from PTSD caused by the incident. I cannot explain why this patient's story and experience affected me the way it did, but I found myself spending more time researching the phenomena. I cultivated a clientele of patients who had similar experiences. All of my psychotherapy sessions dealing with NDE's led me to create my show." The waiter returns with their teas, a tray of milk, cream, and sugar, and a tray filled with different biscuits, jam, butter, and Devonshire cream. He places the teas in front of their respective drinkers, the tray in the center of the table, a small dish in front of each patron, and then leaves the table alone. "The purpose of the show," William continues, "was two-fold: one, to find more people who had experienced NDE's by reaching an audience all over the world and two, to learn more about death, dying, and returning from death."

"There is no returning from death, my friend," Sekhar advises.

"Not true. I've actually seen Death. The entity Death. I've also crossed over while under the administration of drugs and escorting someone who, unintentionally, died."

Rama clarifies, "Dave was a volunteer, yes? Meant to only have a near death experience induced?"

"Yes, but something went wrong and he died. Not before I was able to cross over, though. I saw the afterlife...or part of it, at least. The second attempt confirmed my belief that I had crossed over."

"How so?" Sekhar queries.

"In the first attempt, with Dave, I crossed over with him. I saw what I believed to be part of the afterlife. I saw a room. Dave was in the room, levitating in the center. There were people around him, but they did not appear in a solid state. They were like mist. The room was pretty blank, neutral toned walls, nothing on them. As I looked around the room, I noticed a door with a square window. On the other side of the door, I saw another man looking into the room through the window. He was looking at me. We locked eyes for a moment before I was pulled back into my world. In the second attempt, when I used myself as the test subject, the attempt during which my manager and friend Jakey died, I saw Death come for Jakey. More than that, though, I saw the same man from the afterlife, from my first attempt. He was with Death. He recognized me as well. He appeared like mist, like the people I had seen when I had crossed over during my first attempt. I believe this man is a ghost and that he, for some reason, accompanies Death."

William pauses in his story to take a sip of tea and grab a biscuit. Sekhar watches William closely, concentrating, considering the story he was just told. Rama is quietly drinking his tea and watching Sekhar, eager for his reaction. After a few silent moments, Sekhar returns his cup to the table, leans back, and clasps his hands together in his lap. "It is with no offense that I offer that you are quite possibly mistaken in your beliefs that you have been to the afterlife and seen death."

"What makes you say that?" Rama blurts. "He has compelling evidence and personal experience. Why do you not believe him?"

"What evidence has he? He has told a great ghost story but there is no evidence to speak of in it. He was under the influence of drugs both times he supposedly had these experiences."

"He has EEG's. He has Jakey confirming what Death looks like on film. How can you not consider that evidence?"

"Because he is an educated man that requires definitive proof from multiple sources before he can consider something truth," William states plainly.

"Exactly. Again, Dr. Peters, I mean no offense in my skepticism, but I do not consider a couple of EEG's and the ramblings of a dying man to be evidence of anything, especially considering all were obtained during the commission of a live television broadcast."

"I saw Death a second time. Without drugs. Without cameras."

Rama is surprised by the statement. "I never knew there was a third attempt."

"This wasn't part of a show. It was after my show was cancelled. I started the current research after the cancellation. I went to Egypt, to the Bibliotheca Alexandrina. I spoke with a professor there who is a practicing Kemetic. She sent me to an incense maker in the Cairo marketplace who gave me unabridged copies of the Coffin Texts and The Book of Two Ways. As I was leaving the marketplace, a woman collapsed in the street. I watched her die. I saw Death and the ghost companion again in the marketplace. No drugs. No cameras. No plans."

"You just happened to be there when a random death occurred?"

"Yes. I don't know how it happened, either. I spent my entire journey back to the states trying to figure that out as well. What are the odds?"

Rama whispers in disbelief, "Astronomical, one would guess."

Again, the men pause the conversation to drink tea in silence and mull the contents of the conversation. Sekhar breaks the quiet. "Why do you seek knowledge of Zoroastrianism? I understand your background and your recent attempts, as you call them. What are you trying to accomplish?"

"I have been researching diverse cultural and religious beliefs and practices concerning death and the afterlife. I believe I have stumbled upon a formula. By combining certain beliefs and practices of these cultures and religions, I believe I have figured out a way to find, capture, and destroy death."

Rama looks as surprised as Sekhar upon hearing William's plan. Both men sit stunned as William leans back, smiling, and drinks his tea. William allows time for the men to grasp his words. Sekhar smiles, shakes his head, and then breaks into dismissive laughter. "Death cannot die! It cannot be captured and destroyed. Death is one of the implicit inevitabilities. You are talking nonsense!"

"Death is inevitable only because we do not challenge it. We accept it as inevitable."

"You could spend your whole life believing death to be nothing but smoke and it will still snuff you out eventually. If there were a way to defeat death, do you not believe mankind would have discovered it already? Rama, do you believe in this? I hold no judgments if you do. I hold no judgment of you either, Dr. Peters. I only believe that you are wasting your time in this endeavor, but the time is yours to waste. What aspect of Zoroastrianism do you believe to be part of your formula?"

"If my understanding is correct, your religion believes that the soul or spirit of the deceased remains close to the body for three days and three nights. Is this an accurate understanding?"

"Yes, there is a belief that the spirit suffers its own form of mourning. It is anxious about the departure from the body and the world. It remains during this period as a type of grieving. Once this period is over, the spirit can move on."

Rama interjects, "Why do you focus on this aspect of the religion? How do you think it fits into your plan?"

"The spirit would be the way in."

"In?" Rama repeats, confused.

"To the afterlife. If I know of a Zoroastrian practitioner who has recently passed, I can locate the lingering spirit and cross over with it."

"Then what?" probes Sekhar.

"Find death."

Sekhar scoffs, "Wouldn't you need to locate death before the person has died? I don't think death hangs around after the job is done."

"The incident in the marketplace leads me to believe I can locate death. See, the idea is to locate death, latch on to a spirit before it crosses over, follow it and death into the afterlife, and then capture and destroy death."

"I do not see how this could be possible, but I wish you good luck. Besides, if you are to succeed, then I will be happy to spend countless years telling anyone who will   listen how I sat at this table and helped you to capture and destroy death." The men all laugh and tip their tea cups to each other in a toast to the idea of everlasting life. Sekhar gathers his things, places some money on the table, and gets up from his seat. "I am available to you if you need further information on my religion. If I may offer one last piece of advice?"

"Of course. I am thankful that you have been able to put aside your judgments to assist me. Any advice would be well received."

He places his hand on William's shoulder. "I believe you should ask yourself why you want to destroy death. There is something in you that causes this fear of dying that is leading to your desire to eradicate death. You should think on your true motives. Further, you should ask yourself what kind of world it would be if nothing ever died. Is that world the legacy you want? With that, I bid you both good day. It was a pleasure meeting you, Dr. Peters." William stands up and shakes the hand extended to him by Sekhar. Sekhar nods in Rama's direction. "Rama, I shall see you at the next meeting."

"Of course."

Sekhar walks off down the street. William and Rama both return to their seats and go back to their tea and biscuits. "Do you really think you can do this?" Rama asks tentatively.

"Yes."

"What about the advice offered by Dr. Nimmagadda? What motivates you, do you know?"

"Death hurts people. Losing people, watching people die, what it does to the ones left behind…why wouldn't anyone want to stop that if they could?"

"And what of a world without death?"

"We will adapt just like we've adapted to every new discovery, invention, and scientific breakthrough. We will adapt."

***

Death and Nimitz are at the scene of a bombing. An office building has been destroyed during business hours. Rubble, smoke, blood, and bodies can be seen in the street. First responders rush in all directions, assessing the injured. Nimitz is in shock watching the scene.

"I will stay with you as well if you need me to," Death says to him soothingly.

"No. Do what you need to do. I will be fine. You don't need to expend excess energy staying with me. Be with them."

Death smiles softly at Nimitz, placing her hand next to his face as if she were stroking his cheek. He responds in kind. Then he watches as she disappears from his side and appears in various illuminated forms all around him: angels, cats, dogs, young women, young men, children, birds, clouds. Death appears at the sides of the victims of the tragedy, consoling them as she harvests their souls. Nimitz stands frozen as he watches her, taking in the full scope of what is happening and what she is doing. There are more of her appearing as victims go from critical to deceased. As more of her appear, Nimitz breaks into tears. One form catches Nimitz's eye: an illuminated skeleton. It is unusual to see because he has never seen her appear as anything that could be considered scary. As he watches, the skeleton slowly morphs into a young man.

A voice catches his attention. A young man lain out on the sidewalk is talking to himself. Nimitz walks over to him and realizes how badly the young man is injured. His left leg is missing below the knee. His whole left side is badly burned. He is partially nude as his clothes have either been blown or burned off by the blast. He is not being attended to. Nimitz leans over him. He doesn't know if the man can see him or not, but the man seems to relax some in Nimitz's presence. The young man has a tattoo of a fleur de lis on his right wrist. Nimitz is looking at it intensely as the young man's words filter into his head. "He never could have broken their hearts. He has to know that. It bothers me to think that he doesn't know that. They would have loved him no matter who he chose to love." The fleur de lis brings to mind Heather and

Ferrol. They met in New Orleans. For the first time since he died, Nimitz thinks of his friends. The illuminated figures fade one at a time, the last one at the young man's side, until Death is standing at Nimitz's side again in the form he is used to seeing.

"You were a skeleton. I've never seen you like that. Why that form?"

"Many people fear me. If a dying person is consumed with fear, then I appear in a frightening form. They choose how I appear."

"Then you changed."

"Once she was calm, she was no longer afraid. That shapes me as well."

"This is the first time I have seen you in other forms. In the past when I've accompanied you, I always see you as you are now. I know they see you as something else, but my vision of you has never changed. This time it did. I saw you in all of the different forms. Why?"

"You are starting to accept what I am. Acceptance makes you open. You can see what you were once blind to."

"I feel like I spent my whole life blind to everything around me. Look at what we've done to each other." Nimitz surveys the destruction, saddened.

"Your kind has a tendency to fall into routine. Having that routine upset is usually the first thing to open you up. Another thing is me. Encountering me tends to inspire change, tends to open one's eyes to life. That's what happened with you." Nimitz chokes back tears as Death moves her hand in front of his face.

CHAPTER FOUR

William walks into the room dressed in a suit. The room is filled with people, mostly of Indian descent, silent in prayer. William takes a seat towards the back and remains silent out of respect. At the end of the prayer, the people get up and move around. Some move to a kitchenette area where there are dishes of food and drink. A few walk down a short hall to the room where the body is being viewed.

Sekhar sees William in the back and approaches him. "Dr. Peters. I wasn't expecting to see you here." He extends a hand to William and they shake hands.

"Dr. Nimmagadda, I wish I could say it were under better circumstances. I had to come. He had become a great acquaintance as of late. I was very shocked and sorry to hear of his passing."

"Heart attack. I blame it on his love and adoption of so much Western cuisine." Both men smile uncomfortable smiles at each other. "Have you viewed the body yet?"

"No. I only just arrived during prayers."

"There is a room down the hall where he is laid out. If we were back in India, we would place him outside for the elements and animals to take. Laws prohibit that here, though, so he will be viewed then cremated."

"Won't that upset the lingering spirit?"

"We will still wait three days before cremation. Is that why you're here?"

"There's no point in lying to you. Yes. I am here for two reasons. Rama was a good man and I am here to offer my respects. I am also here to see if I can locate his spirit and cross over with him."

"I would recommend then that you wait until the family has left before you do your viewing. So as not to offend." Sekhar offers his hand again to William, who takes it. Sekhar shakes his hand and then pulls him in close, placing his other hand on William's shoulder. Sekhar whispers into William's ear. "The Center is known for leaving the windows unlocked if you should need to return after hours." Sekhar releases his grip on William and the two men lock eyes.

"Why would you want to help me?"

"You're right. Rama was a good man. And he believed in your work. Goodbye, Dr. Peters."

"Goodbye, Dr. Nimmagadda." William watches him walk out and waits a few minutes before he starts to make his way to the hall. The room is a basic community center classroom that has been cleared of chairs. In the center of the room there is a table. On the table is the body of Rama on a white linen sheet. He is cleaned and formally dressed. William stays in the hall outside the door until he sees the last family member exit. The main hall is almost empty of people when he enters the viewing room. William takes out his cell phone and starts recording.

"This is Dr. William Peters. I am in the Zoroastrian Center where Rama Danasekaran's body has been laid out for viewing. In the Zoroastrian faith, it is believed that the spirit of the recently deceased remains in the area for three days after death. It is my goal to find Rama's spirit, connect with it, and use it to cross over into the afterlife. I am attempting this with no drugs, no assistance, and no crew. I am only recording this attempt for research purposes. Rama Danasekaran. Is your spirit in this room? If so, please send me a sign." William stands in the silent room. There is no movement or noise except for the few remaining attendees in the main hall.

"Rama, this is Will. I would like to know if your spirit is here. In life, you sought to help in my research. In death, you can still provide assistance. Send me a sign." Again, the room is silent and still. William stays very still, looking around the room for any sign of a spirit. The sheet beneath the body moves with the breeze of the air conditioner. William turns towards the door to leave when he hears a loud slam in the room. He looks around the room, but nothing seems to be out of place. He walks along the wall around the room. When he gets to the back of the room, behind the viewing table, he sees a book lying on the floor. The bookshelves against the wall are approximately four feet from the viewing table. William does not recall the book being on the floor when he did his first walk through upon entering. He leans down to inspect the book, to determine if it is his sign, when he notices that it is a copy of the Avesta and it is opened to The Vendidad, one of the major portions of the Avesta that deals with the funeral rituals and the afterlife.

"You're here, Rama. This is the sign. I will return in a few hours once everyone has left. I will be prepared. Do not leave without me." William leaves the room almost running with excitement.

***

Death and Nimitz are at the scene of a multi-car accident. They are both standing on a sidewalk near the cars. "Why are we here?" Nimitz's question perplexes Death.

"I thought it was obvious by now."

"No, I mean, usually when we arrive, you go right to the soul. We've been standing here for a little bit now."

"I did go to a soul when we got here. I wasn't in plain view so you didn't notice as I was also still standing next to you."

"Oh. Then, why are we still here."

"I will be needed shortly."

Nimitz regrets his line of questioning and solemnly apologizes to Death who reassures him that she is aware that he is still learning how all of this works. They remain on the sidewalk together as medical personnel rush around them and people gather on the sidewalks to watch.

***

William crawls in through a window in the viewing room. The Center is empty and dark except for dim night lights in the hallways and the streetlights from outside. Rama's body is still on the table in the center of the room. William pulls a black vinyl duffle bag in through the window. He places it on the floor and opens it up. It contains camera and sound equipment. He does a quick walk through the building to make sure he is alone before he starts unloading and setting up the equipment.

William speaks directly into the camera, "This is Dr. William Peters, Deathhunter. I am currently in a Zoroastrian

Center where the body of my friend Rama is being laid out on view. Earlier today I attended the viewing and, while alone in the room with Rama, I asked if his spirit was still in the room. I received a very clear, very tangible answer to my question so I returned tonight to see if I can cross over with Rama's spirit without the aid of drugs to induce catatonic states. I understand that there is no one here to corroborate what happened or what might happen. I also understand that there is no one that can certify that I am not under the influence of any drugs. I am offering this video as a testament that I have always been truthful in my research and reporting and hope that you, my viewers, will trust that I am still operating with those same principles and ethics now. I have been doing research since my last show. I have travelled to Egypt, India, China, Mexico, and parts of the United States. I have looked into the belief systems of many of the major world religions as well as some arcane and ancient ones to learn more about their views on death and the afterlife. In Egypt, I saw Death. I'm not talking about seeing someone dying. I'm talking about the actual entity of Death. I saw Death in a marketplace in Cairo. Death and its ghostly companion…a man, average looking, nothing special. However, this is the second time I have seen this man with Death. The first time was when Jakey died. Then again in Cairo. When Death visited Jakey, it was a black dog. In the marketplace, Death was a grey cat. I don't know why there is a difference in how Death appears, but it is one of the things that I plan on learning. Tonight, I hope to attach to Rama's spirit and have it carry me over into the afterlife. I have, from the Egyptian religion Kemetism, a book of spells known as The Coffin Texts and a map of the afterlife from the Book of Two Ways. I have located a spell within The Coffin Texts that I believe was meant to attach oneself to a spirit for protection in the afterlife. I have a camera mounted to my glasses and a wireless microphone on my lapel in the hopes that what I experience will be filmed and recorded. Here I go."

William moves over to Rama's body and stands near his head. He lays out the map of the afterlife on the floor at his feet. He stands up straight, opens The Coffin Texts to a bookmarked page and begins reciting the spell, "O, you of the Great Curtain, O, you of the Great West, you beings of the Broad Hall, I speak before you…"

***

Death and Nimitz are now next to an ambulance gurney on the street. Death is bent over a teen-aged girl who is on the gurney. Suddenly, Death quickly turns her head to look at Nimitz. At the same time, Nimitz screws up his face as he feels almost nauseated. He feels his body being pulled. He looks at Death, confused, and reaches for her before he instantly disappears. Death stares at the empty space for a moment, knowingly, before turning her attention back to the girl.

***

William is startled when Nimitz appears in the viewing room. Nimitz is equally startled to see that he has traveled to another location at which he finds the Deathhunter. William continues to recite the spell, "I am here in this land occupying your seat and pulling together your weakness, your companions, bringing up your orphans, strengthening your gate, perpetuating your name upon earth in the mouths of the living…"

Nimitz surveys the scene and becomes anxious. He realizes that there is a body on the table and that the Deathhunter is trying to use it, but Nimitz believes he is trying to call Death to the scene.

"What are you doing?" William's concentration is briefly broken when he hears Nimitz speak, but then he quickly returns to the spell, realizing that it must be working. Nimitz is also surprised to learn that William can hear him.

"…and setting up your door and your tomb at your stairway. Be kindly, be god-like, be god-like, in this sacred land in which you are…"

Nimitz crosses the room to confront William, yelling "Stop!" He slaps the book from William's hand. Both men are surprised to see the book actually slam onto the ground, but William continues to recite the spell, smirking at Nimitz. "When I was in this land of the living, I built your altars, I established your invocation-offerings in your funerary domain which is in the Island of Fire. I heard the word of the Wilful One within the Island of the Living in front of the robing room of the Pure Ones. I shall not perish, I shall not pass away, I shall not die because of them, I shall not die suddenly…"

Before Nimitz can confront him again, Rama's spirit comes into view and then all three disappear together into the blackness. "Not this again," Nimitz laments.

Rama is confused and asks no one in particular, "Where am I?"

William excitedly whispers to himself, "I hope I'm still filming."

A small white dot appears in the center of the darkness. It slowly starts to grow bigger, then it speeds up and the white takes over the entire view. Rama is seated in the chair in the center of The Council Room. He is flanked by William and Nimitz. There is excited and confused murmuring from The Council Members. They are caught off guard by the appearance of three men where there should only be one. The sight is intriguing to the eye: two misty figures and one solid. Rama looks confused. Nimitz looks embarrassed.

William looks victorious. "What is the meaning of this? How are you...Mr. Nimitz? Is that you?" Before Nimitz can respond, the Council Members recognize that William is not deceased. They holds up their hands and, without a word, William disappears from the room. The Council Members then turn to Nimitz and hold up their hands. "We will deal with you momentarily, Mr. Nimitz." Nimitz disappears, mumbling an exaggerated "great" as he does.

***

William looks around the room and realizes where he is. He starts laughing triumphantly before turning his attention to the cameras. "I don't know how much was captured on film or by the mikes, but that was quite an experience. I need to get everything out of here before anyone comes. I will review the footage and update this record."

William packs up the equipment. He gets the book and the map and puts them in the duffle bag before zipping it back up. He walks over to Rama's body and pauses for a moment. "I want to thank you, my friend," William speaks over the body, "for believing in me and supporting me. I also want to thank you for letting me use you as a vessel to cross over. Please know that I am eternally grateful for that favor and for your friendship. Thank you. Go in peace, friend. Goodbye." He crosses to the window, carefully crawls out making sure not to be seen, reaches back in for the duffle bag, and then closes the window.

***

Nimitz appears in the chair where Rama had been. Rama is now gone, off to be hooked up to his eternity. The Council Members appear to be miffed, but calm. They mutter amongst themselves before addressing Nimitz. "Mr. Nimitz, can you explain the circumstances under which you find yourself before us?"

Nimitz hesitates before speaking, trying to determine how much to say. He doesn't want to cause any trouble for Death by admitting she had reached into his eternity to call him out. "I believe I woke up while in my eternity."

"Woke up? Please continue."

"I was in the eternity that you had decided for me. I cannot tell how long I had been in it when I woke up and found myself in the eternity room, fully aware of my situation and its circumstances. I also cannot explain what was drawing me out, but I followed an almost instinctual drive that led me out of my eternity room, down a series of halls, back to the room beneath this chair, up through here, back into the nothingness, and into the realm of the living where I met back up with Death. Again, as time no longer seems to apply, I do not how long I have been away, but I have been acting in a capacity as Death's travelling companion. When I was looking for my way out of here, I stumbled across an eternity room in a dark hallway. I saw a man levitated in the room as I had been in my eternity room. He wasn't alone, though. I saw people, misty in appearance, surrounding him. If I am correct, this is where near death experiences take place. Rooms like that."

"Yes, but this history of yours is not addressing the r…"

Nimitz interrupts, "I wasn't finished. There's much more. While I was looking into the near-death room, I saw a man peeking in from the other side of the room. A living man. The man you expelled from the Council Room a few moments ago." There are collective gasps and murmurs from the Council Members.

"Are you sure of this?"

"Yes. Once I was back in the realm of the living and accompanying Death, I encountered this man again. He is the host of a television show called Deathhunter. The purpose of the show is to investigate near death experiences in the hopes of eventually figuring out how to catch and destroy Death. He was in the middle of one of his live show experiments when I saw him for the first time. The second time I saw him was during his second attempt at crossing over into eternity. That time he also saw Death."

Again, the Council Members murmur, this time a bit louder and more alarmed. "Silence. Please continue."

"He saw Death. The third time I saw him was in a marketplace in Cairo. He saw both of us again. This time, this was the last time."

"This is very concerning, indeed."

"There was something different about this time, though."

"In what way?"

"This time Death was not with me. This time I was literally pulled from where I was to where this man was."

"Explain."

"I was with Death. We were in the city. Multiple car accident. Multiple deaths. One minute I was standing by her side and the next thing I knew, I was being, I don't know how else to explain it, sucked into another place. I looked up and he was there. We were in some classroom or something. The man, the one we came here with, was dead on a table in the center of the room and the Deathhunter was performing some ritual or casting some spell. I guess he was trying to use the man to get here. And I guess it worked. He's not dead. Not even close. And he was here. Has this ever happened?"

"The closest that the living get to eternity is through a near death experience."

"There's more."

"Please continue then."

"He wants to capture and destroy Death. I think he believes Death could be here."

"Death does not exist in eternity."

"You know that. I now know that, but that is not some sort of common knowledge amongst the living. He doesn't know that. He thinks there is a connection between her and eternity because this is where a near death experience brings him. He's going to catch her and kill her."

"Death cannot die."

"Are you so sure of that? Before this man arrived here, you would have said that the living cannot enter eternity."

The Council Members are startled by this statement. "Death cannot die," they repeat.

"That's fine for you to believe. I don't believe that, though, not from what I've seen this man accomplish. How much damage would it do if the living could start entering eternity?"

The Council Members look at each other, considering the weight of the statement. "That is something we have never had to consider…until now. We have always had near death experiences and we have ways of handling that. However, instances of the living fully crossing into eternity…that has never been a consideration."

"I believe it is now. He is broadcasting his experiments. Millions watch him. More will follow him. Where did you send him?"

"We sent him back from whence he came."

"He's after her. I need to get back to her so that I can stop him."

"You wish to register as ghost, then?"

"Yes."

"There are rules."

"There's no time for that."

"Time does not exist here."

"Please…she could be in danger."

"The dead are not allowed to interfere with the living."

"I understand."

"No, Mr. Nimitz, we do not believe that you do. You are asking to go back to stop a living man from killing Death. These are not the statements of a man who believes that he, as ghost, is not going to interfere with the living."

"What is meant by 'interfere' then?"

"Ghosts exist on a separate plane. You can see and be seen, if you so choose. You can communicate, if you so choose. However, you are not allowed to harm the living. You are not allowed to impede life."

"What does that mean? What does impede life mean?"

"Meaning, for example, if you were to witness a child about to be hit by a car, you are not allowed to use your position as spirit to remove the child from the path of the car or to move the car from the path of the child. Understand?"

"Yes. I understand."

"As ghost, spirit, spook, whatever you wish to call it, you can observe, be observed, hear, and be heard. The lines are clear. The rules are simple. The punishment for disobeying is quite severe."

"What is the punishment?"

"Ex-communication. Banishment. Remember the darkness?"

"Yes."

"Imagine if that had pain and profound sorrow."

Nimitz gulps and then chokes out, "Understood. Now, please, I need to get back to her."

"Eternity is not a prison, Mr. Nimitz. You already know how to move through these planes. You are free to leave."

"Thank you." Nimitz gets up from the chair and starts to head to the back wall.

"Mr. Nimitz, one last thing…Her?" Nimitz stops, blushing, and looks into the violet eyes of the Council Members around the room. "We understand love, Mr. Nimitz."

CHAPTER FIVE

William is seated in front of his laptop at the table. A small desk lamp is on, illuminating his face. He is reviewing the video and audio from the Zoroastrian Center. The first video and audio tapes are from during the viewing at the Center. The video shows William and Rama's body, but nothing that translates as a spirit, except the appearance of the book on the floor. The video does not show how the book got on the floor, though. The audio contains William's voice and the echoed murmurs from the main hall. The only other sounds are a few crackles.

Frustrated, William moves on to the video and audio from later when he performed the spell. Immediately, his mood changes. The video clearly shows blurred movement where Nimitz was standing. It shows the blurred image moving towards William. The book appears to be slapped out of William's hand and falls to the floor. Shortly after that, another blurred image appears over Rama's body. Then the two blurred images disappear from the screen leaving William alone in the room. He appears to be in a deep trance. He does not move. He does not even blink. He just stands at the end of the table near Rama's head. The audio features William's voice reciting the spell. It is a constant buzz of words over the ambient environmental noise. William notices the sound cut out. He rewinds the tape and plays it again. Yes, the sound cuts out to complete silence. He notices it again right before the book falls. William, in barely above a whisper to himself, says, "That's when he spoke. The sound cuts out completely when he speaks."

William watches the video for any sign of the afterlife. The video provides nothing except for a few facial reactions to what had been happening. Other than that, it only shows him standing catatonic for almost an hour. The audio, though, contains his voice, cut silences where Nimitz and Rama talked, and a humming noise at the end from when the Council Members were speaking before William was expelled. The end of the video shows William waking up from his catatonic state, gasping loudly for air. For a moment, he looks wildly around the room to determine where he is. Once he realizes he is back in the Center with Rama's body, he places both hands on the ends of the table nearest Rama's head and calms himself. He then turns to the camera and starts laughing. The video ends with him speaking to the camera then turning it off with a huge smile on his face.

William bolts up from his chair and yells out, "I did it!"

***

Death is bedside next to an elderly man when Nimitz appears behind her. She turns to greet him with a serene smile. Nimitz nervously looks around the room. He walks to the door and looks down the halls in both directions. He returns to Death's side, she puts her hand in front of his face, and they find themselves on an empty beach. Nimitz looks around, not seeing any living beings.

"Why are we here?"

"I figured that you might need to talk and I know you find this place comforting."

"How do you know that?"

"This was chosen as your eternity for a reason. Your soul was most at peace here."

"I never thought about it, but I guess some of the best times of my life were spent on this shore."

"Did you speak to The Council?"

"Yes, I talk...wait, you know that I went back?"

"Yes. You were pulled. I knew it must be The Council calling you to task for not registering as a ghost."

"I did go before The Council and we did discuss that, yes, but that isn't what pulled me away."

"It wasn't?"

"No. I was pulled to some empty classroom with that man, the Deathhunter, and the body of a dead man in it. The Deathhunter was reciting some spell or something from some book and, next thing I knew, the dead man's spirit was there and we were all being pulled into the nothingness. Then we were in the Council Room. The Council sent the Deathhunter back to the classroom where we had come from and they sent me to my eternity room.

When they called me back, the dead man was gone and we discussed everything that has happened: me escaping my eternity, finding you...don't worry I didn't tell them that you showed up in my eternity or called me out of it."

"Benjamin, you are adorable. When are you ever going to understand that I don't get into trouble? I shouldn't have done what I did, calling you out, but it's not like The Council can punish me."

"I don't know all the rules, so I figured I would leave you out of it. Anyway, I told them about the Deathhunter, about his plan to infiltrate eternity and destroy, well, you."

"And what was their reaction?"

"They were concerned about the fact that a living being made it all the way into eternity."

"They should be concerned about that. Of course, the living should be concerned about that as well, but it's not possible to tell them that. Did you register as ghost?"

"Not that I am aware of, but The Council knows it is my intention to stay with you and we did review the rules. We kept it brief as I was concerned about your safety…hush, I know…and I wanted to get back to you."

"I'm glad you're back. They registered you then. If rules were reviewed then you are fine to be in the realm of the living. I just want you to completely understand the severity of breaking those rules, though. Considering how concerned you are about this death hunter, I want to make sure you understand that you cannot interfere in any way."

"I understand the rules and, despite being worried about your safety, I trust that you can defend yourself. I will remember the rules if I ever find myself face to face with the Deathhunter again."

"I would hate to lose you."

"You won't."

***

William is sitting in front of his laptop with the camera on. He is speaking to the camera and recording. "First, before I

crossed over, death's ghostly companion
appeared in the room at the Zoroastrian
Center. He was angry at what I was
attempting to do and attempted to stop me
from reciting the spell by knocking the book
out of my hands. Then, Rama's spirit
appeared and we all crossed over together:
Rama, me, and the ghost. Everything went
black and I could no longer tell if I had a
body or if I was alone. I couldn't see
anything and the only thing I could hear
was my own voice, although even that
could have just been my thoughts. A small
white dot appeared and it slowly grew
bigger until it started speeding up and took
over all the space around me. It was
extremely bright so it took my eyes a few
seconds to adjust. Once I could see again, I
was in a round white room. All along the
walls were chairs, forming a circle around
where I was standing. In the chairs were
men and women wearing white robes. They
all had violet eyes. They were definitely
surprised to see me there. I was standing
next to a chair that was bolted to the floor in
the center of the room. In the chair was
Rama. Standing on the other side of Rama
was death's ghostly companion. He also
seemed upset at being there. Before
anything could happen, one of the men in

the white robes held up his hand in my direction and I was blasted back into my body in the Zoroastrian Center. My video and audio footage do not show any of this, even though I was wearing camera-fitted glasses and a microphone. I don't know how I am going to do it, but I am determined to film it somehow. Next time I cross over, there will be evidence of the afterlife. As always, thank you for your support, believers. Until next time…"

William waves at the camera before shutting it off and saving the video. He looks at the clock, noting the time, and closes his laptop. He moves from the table to an area in the front of the warehouse set up like a living room. He gets to work setting up cameras and lighting. He hooks up his laptop to the cameras. He lays out the map from The Book of Two Ways on a coffee table in the center of the room. He sets The Coffin Texts on the side table next to a couch. Next to that he sets his copy of The Avesta. He goes to his office table and rummages in a medium sized box on top of it. He takes out a few small infrared cameras and unpackages them. He lays them out gently on the table. He does the same with some microphones. He steps back and surveys the scene in the office and the living room. Satisfied with this, he orders himself some takeout and then jumps into the shower.

      He showers, shaves, and wraps up in a robe. He walks into the kitchen and makes himself a cup of tea. While the tea is steeping on the counter, a buzzer sounds. William walks to the front door, opens it, and signs for his takeout food. He goes back into the kitchen, opens the takeout containers, makes himself a plate of Chinese food, grabs the cup of tea and the plate, and goes back into the living room. He sits down on the couch, turns on the television, and watches some mindless sitcom as he eats his food. He takes his time eating, savoring the food. Once he is finished eating and drinking his tea, he puts his dishes away. He walks back into the bathroom and brushes his teeth, combs his hair, and gets dressed. He wears a nice pair of black pants with a nice dress shirt tucked in. Black dress shoes and a black leather belt complete the outfit. He walks over to the office table and puts one of the cameras on his glasses frame, another on his lapel, and he saves one to carry in his hand. He attaches one microphone to his other lapel and one to a wrist band on his hand. He goes back into the living room and turns on the cameras. He is now live streaming. William steps into frame. He looks directly into the camera.

"Good evening, believers. I come to you tonight from my own home. It occurred to me the other night that people die every day. Thousands of them. This thought led me to the idea that I don't need to create a situation in which someone is put under and opened up to a near death experience or seek out a situation in which someone is dying or recently deceased. No. I should be able to use the skills I've learned from my research to attach myself to any dying being without actually having to go out and find it. I should be able to project myself from here and attach to the dying soul as it crosses over. Tonight, I will make such an attempt. I am prepared for what may come. If I do not make it back, let this broadcast serve as my final goodbye. Thank you for supporting me. Hopefully, I will see you soon on the other side. Let's cross over and hunt Death!"

William steps back to the center of the room. He picks up The Coffin Texts and starts reciting the spell.

Nimitz places his hands on his stomach. He recognizes the feeling. He is about to be sucked away again. Death turns to look at him and gives him a consoling smile before he disappears.

Nimitz appears in the hallway. He looks around and recognition shows on his face. He knows where he is, but not why. The last time he was pulled away was to meet the Deathhunter. The confusion turns to anger when he sees the Deathhunter sneaking down the hall towards him. William is in a trance. He is still mindlessly chanting the spell, but he is not fully awake. The spirit of an elderly Indian woman appears in the room, looking scared and confused. William smiles at her and they both disappear.

"Blackness," William whispers. "I remember this. Next will be that white room. Need to move fast to get out of that room."

The elderly woman speaks to herself, "Is this heaven or hell? Is this it? This isn't so bad, I guess."

The small white dot appears, growing larger then speeding up to take over the blackness. The elderly woman is seated in the chair. William notices a hole in the floor of the room. He realizes that the chair is about to move over it, so he lets go of the chair, slides to the floor, and slips into the hole. He jumps down into the control room through the hole in the floor. He looks around, sees no one, and runs through the door.

William looks down the hallway and, still not seeing anyone, slowly makes his way down. He looks into the windows as he passes, holding the camera up to them, and narrating what he is seeing as he goes. He is so focused on what he is doing that he doesn't notice Nimitz at the end of the hallway. Nimitz waits for William to get close to him. He is seething, but is reminding himself of the rules. Do they apply here? They are in eternity, after all. William is startled when he sees Nimitz. Both men stand opposite each other, staring. William holds up the camera to film Nimitz.

"How did you get here?"

"Research."

"Yes, you are just brilliant, aren't you?"

"If you say so. So, what's your deal? Are you a ghost? Death's lackey? What?"

"You have to leave."

"I'll leave when I'm caught and told to leave."

"Consider yourself caught and told."

"You don't really seem threatening. I don't feel threatened by you." William starts walking towards Nimitz, pausing next to him to stare him in the eyes close up. He puts the camera right in front of Nimitz's face. "Smile."

Nimitz is livid, his cheeks flush with anger, but he remains still as William walks past him and down the next hall. Nimitz concentrates on the Council Room and suddenly finds himself there. None of the Council Members are in the room, so he approaches one of the doors behind the chairs. He knocks on the door, surprising himself with his own forcefulness. When no one answers, he opens the door. The inside of the Council Member's room is soft white, comforting. It is set up like an eternity room except it has a less clinical feel to it. The only other difference is that the Council Member levitates standing up rather than lying down. Nimitz hesitates to speak, afraid that a sudden jolt from hearing someone in the room will somehow hurt the Council Member.

"What brings you back here, Mr. Nimitz?"

Nimitz is startled. "How did you…"

"We have the ability to pick up energy levels. Every energy level is unique, identifying the being to which it belongs. We recognized you as soon as you knocked on the door."

"Then why didn't you respond?"

"We wanted to see if you would give up or persevere."

"I thought you should know that the Deathhunter is loose in eternity."

"That is impossible."

"Apparently not because I was drawn here and there he was, walking down the halls, looking into the windows of the eternity rooms, and filming."

The Council Member descends, moves towards Nimitz, and holds his hand up before Nimitz's face. Nimitz finds himself transported to The Council Room with all the Council Members in their seats.

They murmur seriously amongst themselves.

"What are we going to do?" Nimitz asks them.

"You will do nothing. We are going to expel him like before."

"That's not going to stop him. He'll just keep coming back."

"We cannot stop him from trying to enter eternity. We can only expel him when he does. He poses no threat."

"You said this had never happened before. You said that a living being had never fully entered eternity before. This man has now done it twice. Three times if you count when I first saw him just peeking in from the outside. Obviously, there is something special about this man that makes it possible for him to see the dead, see Death herself, and enter eternity. That doesn't concern you? What if he shuts everything down in here? What if all the souls here in eternity are awakened and sent back to the living realm to operate as ghosts? Wouldn't that be an issue?"

"Mr. Nimitz, the security of eternity is none of your concern. We managed to exist long before your arrival and we shall exist long after. While this has never occurred before, it does not mean it is cause for alarm. What should be concerning you is your connection to this man."

"What do you mean by that? I have no connection to him."

"It occurs to us that every time he has entered eternity, you have been involved."

Nimitz opens his mouth to respond, but then it hits him that it is true. He ponders this for a moment, trying to determine why this man has a connection to him and what it means, when the orderlies appear in the Council Room.

"There is a trespasser. He has entered one of the eternity rooms," the first orderly informs them.

"Do you know which one?"

The second orderly responds, "Yes. We have it on the map."

The Council Member holds his hand up in the air and William appears in the chair. William looks upset, not at all the inflated, confident man that Nimitz is used to seeing as of late. The Council Members stare at him, concentrating on him. "Dr. William Caleb Peters, what has brought you here?"

"How do you know my name?"

"We know everything." Nimitz looks at the Council Members, puzzled. If this statement is true, then that would mean that they knew he had escaped his eternity, that this man had entered, and what he was doing there. William apparently had the same thought.

"If you know everything, then you know what brought me here and how I got here."

"We do."

"Then why are you asking me?"

"Everything is measured, including how you respond to answered questions."

"I'm here to find and destroy death."

"Death does not exist in eternity and death cannot die."

"I shouldn't exist in eternity either, yet here I am. Alive."

"This does not change our response."

"What are you doing with these people here?"

"We do not have to explain anything to you."

"If this is the afterlife, it looks like a prison. Who the hell would want to spend eternity hooked up to machines in a prison cell?"

"You presume to understand things that you have only witnessed in passing. That can be dangerous. You do not belong here, Dr. Peters. You must return to your realm."

"I will just keep coming back until I get what I want."

"We know." The Council Members lift their hands and William disappears, but not before he once again gives Nimitz a creepy sideways smirk. The Council Members then turn their attention back to the orderlies. "Was anything disturbed?"

"Not that we could see," advises the second orderly.

The second orderly further informs, "We did a full scan."

"Thank you. You may both go."

The orderlies disappear. Nimitz is trying to process everything that has happened: him being connected somehow to William; William having the ability to see him, the dead, and Death; William having the ability to enter eternity at will; William having entered one of the eternity rooms; the Council Members knowing about all of this yet doing nothing.

"As was previously stated," the Council Members say, "we have always secured eternity and will continue to do so. Dr. Peters can see death. So can you, Mr. Nimitz. Many people are able to see the dead. As for his adventures in eternity, we cannot explain how he is able to enter, but we know he is no threat. His connection to you is curious, but we do not care enough to consider it any further. Have you any questions?"

"Literally millions, but, as you so eloquently put it, I do not care enough to consider them any further." Nimitz smiles plaintively at the Council Members before he disappears.

***

William is poring over the audio and video footage. He looks like he hasn't slept in days. He is unshaven, bleary-eyed, and his clothes are rumpled and dirty. On the table next to his laptop are takeout boxes from a variety of restaurants. He repeatedly starts, stops, rewinds, and restarts the footage in different places. The video shows William standing in his living room. He is catatonic. This scene stays static for a while and William forwards past it until the screen goes black. The sound of William's voice can be heard in the darkness. "Blackness. I remember this. Next will be that white room. Need to move fast to get out of that room."

There are a few seconds of complete silence. The normal white noise of audio is even missing. The screen stays black as William forwards past it. The screen suddenly turns all white for just a flash. Then it goes beige. Various thumps and movement noises can be heard on the audio as the screen goes from light beige to a darker shade of beige. As the screen changes color, the sound of a door closing can be heard. William forwards past some of the beige screen, stops, does a short rewind, and then plays the video. The screen is still beige, but there is dialogue.

"Research."

There is a second of the same complete silence.

"If you say so. So, what's your deal? Are you a ghost? Death's lackey? What?"

Complete silence.

"I'll leave when I'm caught and told to leave."

Complete silence.

"You don't really seem threatening. I don't feel threatened by you."

A few seconds of complete silence. The sound of movement.

"Smile."

William forwards past more beige screen then stops. There is the sound of a gasp, then stressed breathing. There is the sound of a door opening. The screen lightens, but is still beige. There is the sound of a door closing. A few seconds of stressed breathing. In the center of the screen is a small blur.

William, his voice strained, cries, "Caleb? Oh my God, Caleb. What are they doing to you? Oh my God. I miss you so much. You and mommy. I miss you both so much. I'm so sorry, Cay. I should be here. Not you. Never you. Not mommy. Not you. I'm so sorry, little man. I miss you so much, Cay. So much. I'm going to have to go now, Cay. I can't stay. I want to, but they're going to kick me out of here soon as they find out where I am. I'll be back, though, Caleb. I'll be back to visit you and mommy. Is Mommy around here? She's got to be close by. She's got to be here, too. What have they done to you, little man?" William can be heard crying, then sniffling as he composes himself. "Okay, I have to go now. I love you, little man. I love you, Caleb. Daddy loves you, Cay. I do."

William stops the video. Crying, he lays his head down on the table for a moment before starting the video again. He forwards past more beige screen. Stops. The screen is light beige. There is a blur in the center of the screen again, but this one is larger. More stressed breathing. "Oh God, Viv. Vivvie." There is a sound indicating that William has fallen to the ground as the point of view of the blur sinks. "Viv.

Forgive me, Viv. I need to know you forgive me. I miss you so much, Vivian. I saw Cay. I saw our son. I don't know what's going on, Viv. I think I might be losing it. I don't know if you're really here. I don't know if I'm hallucinating. Viv, I don't sleep well. I mean, you know I was always energetic, but now it's different. I don't sleep now because I don't like waking up alone. I miss you guys. You and Cay, you never should have died. It shouldn't have been you guys. If I had been home…Oh Viv, please forgive me." The sounds of William crawling across the floor can be heard underneath his low sobs as the blur grows larger and almost takes up the whole screen. "I'm working hard, Viv. I'm working on something that will change the world. It will change life. You would be so proud of me, Vivvie. I miss you, Viv." The blur returns to the original position in the center of the screen as the sound of William standing up can be heard.

"I have to go, Vivian. I don't want to, but I can't stay here. I'll come back. I promise. I love you, Viv. Always. Still. I love you, Vivvie. Goodbye." William pauses the video and tenderly touches the blur on the screen before he breaks down again.

***

"The Council believes that the Deathhunter is connected to me rather than you. William. His name is William."

"That is more probable."

"Why do you say that?"

"You are of the same kind. You spent a lot of your time around the dying. Your profession required it. That and your solitary life made you open to seeing me. The Deathhunter has also spent quite a bit of his time around the dying. He also, I assume, leads a rather solitary life. He saw you before he saw me. That is probably where the connection was made."

"He's not hunting me."

"No, but he connected with you and the connection is apparently strong enough for you to be drawn to his location as you were drawn to mine when you were living."

"He's hunting you through me."

"Yes."

"I'm the one putting you in danger."

"I'm in no danger."

***

The screen is white with several blurs appearing in a circular pattern.

William's voice can be heard saying, "If you know everything, then you know what brought me here and how I got here."

Humming noise.

"Then why are you asking me?"

Humming noise.

"I'm here to find and destroy death."

Humming noise.

"I shouldn't exist in eternity either, yet here I am. Alive."

"It goes on like this for a minute or two more. You can hear my part of the conversation, but, when they speak, all you hear is that humming noise." William points at the frozen laptop screen of white with the blurs on it. He indicates the blurs. "These.

These blurs. These are spirits. They appear as humans in that realm. They speak as one. They were different ages, races, sexes. They all wore white robes and had violet eyes. They appear on film as blurs, but those are spirits!"

Sekhar is seated at the table. He is closely studying the image on the screen, but he appears unconvinced. He looks at William with a concerned eye. "When did you last sleep, my friend?"

"That's got nothing to do with it! I was there! I saw it all! This footage is proof."

"This footage is proof of nothing concrete."

"You've never been a believer. Rama would have seen this for what it truly is: proof of life after death."

"Your invocation of Rama's name does nothing to sway me. I know what you're attempting and, I admit, you've a very entertaining story with excellent imagery and theatrics with the video. It is not, however, anything concrete. This is the type of thing that could have been done alone with editing software."

William, defeated, but unrelenting, mutters, "It wasn't. It's real."

"What do you plan to do with this? What is next?"

"This was a live stream. It's already out there. My analysis is still being completed, but, once it is done, it will be uploaded as well. My supporters, my believers, will see it for what it is."

"My friend, what is the end game here?"

"I'm going after death next."

CHAPTER SIX

William is standing in a section of the warehouse that is separated from the rest of the warehouse by walls. It is a smallish room that was once an office. It is dark. In the center of the room is a plexiglass cage kind of like the ones on game shows where people stand inside and try to catch dollar bills as they fly around. Written on each of the walls are texts in different languages: Arabic, Spanish, Hindi, Haitian Creole, and Latin. On the walls of the room outside of the cage are symbols from many different languages and texts. There are infrared cameras and microphones mounted all over the room at different angles. William takes out a small remote and pushes a button, activating the cameras and microphones.

"Tonight, dear believers, I am going to attempt to bring death here. I have created an environment in which death can be contained. I have spells that are meant to summon death. The idea is to summon death into this room, trap it in this cage, and destroy it. There are spells and symbols meant to contain, harm, or stave off death written on the cage and the walls around it.

I have other spells that are also meant to hurt death. In my research, I have come across a number of spells and rituals that are meant to stop or destroy death. I have also discovered spells and rituals that will render death's ghostly companion harmless. I have studied the research for years. I am confident that I can summon death, capture it, and destroy it. As always, I thank you all for your continuing support and faith in me. You all know what comes next. Let's cross over and hunt Death!"

William steps away from the camera and begins reciting spells. "I am he whose knife is sharp, who went out into the day and who has power over his foes: a way has been given to me, I have power in my legs, I come out into the day against my foe, I have power over him, even as He whose shape is invisible commanded." While reciting, he also spreads ash in a circle on the ground around the cage. In each corner of the room, there is a small wooden stand. On each stand, there is a brass bowl filled with dried sage. William walks from one corner to the other and recites an incantation over each bowl while lighting hide wrapped bones on fire and placing them into the bowls. He stands still and chants as though he is in a trance. "I have come here from the Tribunal, my affair has been judged with it, and I am vindicated. A way has been given to me by Him whose shape is invisible; he has taken the breath from my nose before my days had come and he has brought me to this place, my food being on earth and my magic in my ritual incantations, so that he might bring to me my foe, and I have power over him, even as He whose shape is invisible commanded."

Nimitz feels the familiar pull in his stomach. It isn't strong, but it is there. He knows he's about to be pulled to William's location. While it is a now familiar thing, he still gets nervous when it happens because he doesn't know what to expect. He keeps his eye on Death, waiting for her to turn around, but instead she stands upright very quickly, looks around wildly, and disappears. Nimitz is alone on the mountain. He starts to mildly panic for a moment before he remembers that he can find her by concentrating on her. He stands still on the mountainside, closes his eyes, and concentrates.

Death appears inside the plexiglass cage. She looks around, confused, for a moment before she sees William standing in the shadows. She watches as William starts walking around the cage. To him, she appears as black smoke. Nimitz appears in the room, but he is outside the cage. Before he can adjust to his new surroundings, William sees him and starts an incantation meant to incapacitate him.

"The vindication of a man against his foes is brought about in the realm of the dead." Nimitz feels weak and falls to his knees, looking at Death with fear in his eyes. Once Nimitz is on the ground, William, satisfied, turns his attention back to Death.

William throws his hands into the air and starts reciting a spell. "Ho, there will come to you those who come to Horus who dwells in his house on that day when all the gods were clothed at the burial of Osiris and of that day of interment. Ho, those who wept for Osiris will weep for you on that day…" Death writhes in the cage, turning into a fine, black mist like sand in a storm. Nimitz reaches out to the cage. "No! Stop! You're hurting her!"

"Her?" William looks back into the cage and then back at Nimitz with a wild look in his eye. "Death is a 'her'?"

Nimitz begs, "Please stop."

William stares right into Nimitz's eyes before he continues the spell, louder this time, with more zeal. "Ho, those who mourned Osiris will mourn you on that day of the sixth-day festival in which the gods swooned. Ho, Horus himself will cleanse you in that pool of cold water. Ho, Anubis the embalmer will enwrap you with wrappings from the hand of Tayt!" The fine, black mist that is Death settles to the floor of the cage. Nimitz, grief-stricken at what he believes is the end of Death, focuses on one the brass bowls in the corner.

Nimitz warns, "I may not be able to touch you, but that doesn't mean I can't hurt you."

The brass bowl flies at William's head. William ducks just before the bowl smashes into him. The other three follow suit. One catches William on the forehead, knocking him back against a wall for a moment and cutting him. He stands back up and begins again. "Ho, Anubis the embalmer has mummified you with his best embalming. Thoth will cleanse for you the fair paths of the West to Osiris!" This one raises Death into the air in the cage and binds her. The mist is tightly packed within a braid of twine, suspended in the air. William looks over his shoulder at Nimitz, triumphant.

"This has just been child's play, here. Now I'm going to get serious. You might want to prepare yourself."

Nimitz is emboldened by this statement. He stands up and focuses all of his energy on the wall behind William. The wall begins to shake, then creak, before the boards give way and fly inward towards William with alarming speed and ferocity. William turns in time to be slammed by the boards and he falls to the floor, covered in wooden rubble. Nimitz moves towards the cage, but stops short when he hears Death speak.

"Step away, Benjamin."

"But I can get you out of there. I can save you."

Death, in an increasingly deep, angry voice, commands, "I told you that I do not need protecting. Remember what I am. Step away now!"

The sound of the boards moving behind him causes Nimitz to look back at William, who is slowly getting himself out from under the rubble and to his feet. He is a bit shaky and pale.

"Now, Benjamin!"

William, breathlessly, mocks, "Yeah, Benjamin. Step away."

Nimitz backs away until he is against a wall, confused. A shrieking noise leaves him wide-eyed as he sees Death transform into something terrifying. William is struck silent and frozen. The plexiglass cage breaks into pieces as the fine, black mist bound in twine becomes solid and grows, filling the room with its substantive shape. Death is a thirty foot banshee creature draped in black, smoke-like robes, with a long, misshapen face. There are deep, black, sunken holes where the facial features should be. The smooth black skin that Nimitz is used to seeing turns grey and cracks, dried and decomposing. The creature reaches out to William with elongated, thin fingers. William puts his hands over his ears to dull the shrieks coming from it. Death moves towards William slowly, but menacingly.

William creeps back from the dark room into the open area of the warehouse. With a wave of her arms, the internal walls of the room are blown apart. Nimitz follows them, keeping a distance between himself and the scene.

"You! You tiny man! You dare to believe that you are going to capture me, to tame me? You think you are the first to attempt to destroy me? You only have the knowledge because there were others before you. Greater men! Smarter men! Braver men! Do you see them here? No! Do you see me? Fool! I cannot die. I AM DEATH! You were so convinced that you would be triumphant! You were so arrogant reciting those spells, but you were only playing. Like a little boy with his daddy's tools. You think you know what it is, but not how it is used. Faith, William. Those rituals, symbols, and spells are used for faith. They are used to help those who believe to feel they have control, to lose their fear of me, because they choose how I appear to them. You have no faith, William. You only have fear and anger. Fear and anger manifest me in terrifying ways."

William is now backed into a corner, cowering, with Death towering over him.

"Where is your bravery now, William? Where is your arrogance?"

Shaking visibly and stammering, William cries out, "You can't touch me!"

"Oh, can't I?" Death taunts, hovering a finger just above William's head.

"No! There are rules. You cannot just harvest the souls of those who try to trap you, hurt you, or who just piss you off."

As William gains back his confidence, Death starts to transform again. Shrinking down in size and taking on the appearance of a small boy. William gasps and collapses again, sobbing. "This is why you are angry, isn't it, William? You think I took them from you and that broke your heart."

"It should have been me," William whispers through his tears, his head in his hands, unable to look at the child before him.

"It wasn't you who summoned me."

"What do you mean?"

"I don't choose who dies. I am summoned when I am needed. You were not the one who summoned me. Vivian and Caleb did. That would not have changed had you been home that night."

"They wouldn't have gone out. Caleb was sick. If I had been home, I could have gone to get his medicine and Vivian would not have had to put him in the car to go herself. They would have been home."

Death transforms again into a softer form, almost angelic. Kneeling down and looking into William's eyes, she tells him, "They still would have summoned me. The only thing it would have changed is the manner by which they came to me."

William looks into Death's eyes and breaks down, finally acknowledging that there was nothing he could have done to save his wife and child. Quietly, he tells Death, "I miss them so much."

"I know. You grew so angry that you convinced yourself that you could eradicate me from existence, preventing anyone else from ever having to experience the pain of loss that you did. It was a noble thought, William, despite its selfish origination. You were trying to spare the world of pain, but, in the process, yours grew so large that it consumed you. Have you figured out why I appeared here tonight?"

"Yes."

"You summoned me, William."

"I know."

"You knew it was time."

"I believe I did."

"Are you ready now?"

"Will I see them again?"

"That I cannot know."

"You will." Both William and Death look at Nimitz, startled by his comment.

"How can you know that?" William asks.

"The Council will choose your eternity based on you. You'll spend eternity with them. I promise you will."

William looks from Nimitz to Death. He looks around the room, closes his eyes, takes a deep breath, and says, "I'm ready."

"Let go."

As William's body goes limp against the wall, he looks at Nimitz, then at

Death, smiles a genuinely contented smile, and whispers, "Thank you."

Nimitz looks at Death. "I want to go with him. I will come back."

"I understand. Go."

William is in the chair. Nimitz stands next to him. The Council Members seem a bit surprised to see Nimitz again, especially considering whom he is accompanying. "Mr. Nimitz. You are becoming something of a regular sight in this room. Will you please excuse us?"

"I'd like to stay if that is acceptable to the Council."

"These proceedings are not for public entertainment. You may not stay."

"I would like to testify on his behalf."

"What curious wording. He is not on trial here, Mr. Nimitz. You are aware of that, seeing as how you've been in that chair before. He does not need your testimony. We already know what you know."

"Of course. In that case, might I be able to wait and speak with you afterwards?"

"That is acceptable."

"Would it also be acceptable for me to accompany William to his eternity room?"

The Council Members confer quietly. "That is also acceptable."

"Thank you." Nimitz nods his head at William, then at the Council Members, before he disappears.

"We welcome you, Dr. William Caleb Peters. Have you any questions?"

***

The orderlies escort William into the hall.

"I can take him from here," Nimitz advises. The orderlies offer no opposition. They turn around and head back into the Control Room beneath the Council Room. Nimitz and William start walking down the hall.

"Does it hurt?"

"Not as much as a wall caving in on you. Sorry about that, by the way, but you were being a bit of an ass."

"I was. I understand so much more now."

"Sadly, that seems to be the way it works here. We learn so much that we should have known when we were among the living."

"Why are you being so nice since I was being such an asshole?"

"Death is a woman. To me, anyway. I fell in love with her before I ever realized what she was. She fell in love with me as well. Weird, I know. I never knew anger like the anger you've carried with you. The closest I've come is when she was almost taken away from me. I understand now where your anger originated. While I cannot say I've known pain that deep, I can say that I understand why you were that angry. It changed the way I saw you just like it changed the way Death appeared to you. You don't need more anger."

"I appreciate that. Thank you."

Nimitz stops in front of a door. "This is you. If I am correct, Vivian and Caleb are on either side of you."

William chokes back tears as they enter the eternity room. Nimitz levitates him and gets him hooked up.

"You should be with them soon. It will be nice. It's not prison. It truly is an eternity in peace."

"Why didn't you stay in yours?"

"She's my eternity. It was nice meeting you, Dr. Peters."

"It was nice meeting you as well, Benjamin."

Nimitz pushes the final button as William slips into his eternity.

***

Nimitz stands before the Council Members.

"You wished an audience with us, Mr. Nimitz?"

"Yes. Thank you for obliging me."

"Before we turn the floor over to you, we wanted to thank you for your dedication to the protection of eternity and to Death. While you must now understand that neither were ever in any true danger, we respect that you were willing to face the danger you perceived in our name. For that, we owe you a debt of gratitude."

"Funny you should say that you owe me a debt…"

"Is it?"

"I have a request of The Council. An unusual request, but one that I believe can be granted without exceeding any bounds or breaking any rules."

"Do go on."

"I'd like to request that I be allowed to…"

***

Nimitz stares at a television screen through the window of an electronics store. It is showing a news report on the death of a celebrity.

"Millions of people all over the world were shocked today to learn of the death of Dr. William Peters who was also known as The Deathhunter. Dr. Peters, on one of his missions to capture and destroy death, died of a heart attack on live broadcast online. Dr. Peters was preceded in death by his wife, Vivian, and his son Caleb, fifteen years ago when they both died in a car accident. It was around that time that Dr. Peters started focusing solely on dealing with near death experiences. That research led to his show, The Deathhunter, which became an enormous success nearly overnight. Of course, it wasn't without controversy, especially with the live shows that ended up broadcasting two real deaths: that of a volunteer only known as Dave and that of Jacob Schmidt, Dr. Peter's manager, who was affectionately known as Jakey. Overall, the show worked to help people and, in his career both on and off screen, Dr. Peters helped thousands of people. He will be missed."

Nimitz smiles at the sentiment put forth by the broadcast as he turns to greet Death. "Can we pop by Peaks Island? There's something I want to show you."

Death looks quizzically at Nimitz, wondering what he is up to, but obliges him by raising her hand in front of his face.

Death and Nimitz stand on the beach by the water's edge. Nimitz takes in the sky, the water, the dunes, and the air. He can clearly recall how each feels, smells, and sounds. He smiles broadly, looking into Death's dark eyes.

"Kiss me," he finally says.

"What?"

"Kiss me."

"Benjamin, you know that I can't do that. We've talked about this."

"About that…I talked with The Council and we made an agreement."

"What kind of agreement?"

"I can touch you, but only for a second or two. After that, I will disintegrate or burst into dust or something along those lines."

Death looks horrified, so Nimitz quickly reassures her. "Painlessly! Completely painlessly!"

"So, I get one kiss and then I get to watch you disintegrate?"

"Yes, but there's more."

Death sarcastically replies, "Oh good!"

"I will regenerate."

"What?"

"I can touch you for only a second or two, just long enough for a kiss, but then I will disintegrate. Then I will regenerate. This way, I can at least be able to give you a kiss, which I would like to do now."

"The Council...they agreed to this?"

"Yes. It was their way of thanking me for being concerned with the safety of eternity."

"This was your idea, though?"

"Yes, it was. After almost losing you, or thinking that I was going to lose you, I could not shake the feeling that I would never know what it would feel like to hold you or kiss you. That's all I need. I just want to know that I can hug you or hold your hand, touch your face or kiss your lips. Even if just for a moment."

Their faces barely an inch apart, they both look into each other's eyes, smile, and blush like two teenagers contemplating their first kiss. Nimitz studies Death's features, realizing that she looks a bit different from their first meeting. She's more familiar to him now, like he's staring into the face of someone he's known for years and seeing them anew.

"Benjamin?"

"Yes?"

"Kiss me."

Nimitz leans all the way in and passionately kisses her, wrapping his arms around her as he does. Within seconds, he begins to illuminate. He bursts into stardust rising into the night sky. Death stands on the shore, smiling at the starlit sky, and watches him disappear.

CHAPTER SEVEN

Nimitz's vision is blurred, but he can just make out the darkened figure of Death standing over him. "See, I told you I would regenerate," he says triumphantly.

"Ben?"

"Death?"

"What? Ben!" The darkened figure moves away as Nimitz's vision clears. "Nurse! He's awake!"

The figure returns, but Nimitz recognizes that it is not Death. The room comes into more focus. He's in a hospital, in the bed. The voice he heard belongs to Ferrol who is standing at his bedside talking. Nimitz cannot focus on his words just yet as he is still processing his surroundings. Ferrol just sounds like a hum in his ear. Sensing his confusion, Ferrol stops talking and just stands next to his friend's bed as the nurses and a doctor rush into the room.

"Mr. Nimitz," the doctor addresses him, "do you know where you are?"

"What? Who are you? Where's Death?"

"I'm sorry, sir, did you ask for death?"

"Yes. Where is she? I was told I would be returned to her when I regenerated. This wasn't part of the deal!"

"Mr. Nimitz, sir, my name is Dr. White. You are at Cornell Medical Center. Do you know why you're here?"

Nimitz goes limp against the bed, silent. He cannot remember anything before dying. He looks around the room for Ferrol. For anyone that he recognizes. For anything that he recognizes. He catches sight of Ferrol by the door. He's upset. It looks like he's been crying. *I'm in love with him.* He hears Ferrol's voice in his head. He and Ferrol make eye contact as the realization hits Nimitz that it was Ferrol. The old woman in the Cairo marketplace was talking, but they were Ferrol's words. Before he can say anything, Dr. White steps into his line of vision.

"Mr. Nimitz, do you know why you're here?"

Defeated and confused, Nimitz answers, "No. No, I don't. I don't know what's happening."

Dr. White takes out a penlight and examines Nimitz's eyes. "You were electrocuted, sir. Do you remember being electrocuted?"

"What? No. No, that's not how I died. Is it?"

"Sir, you were electrocuted, but you did not die. You were in a coma. Do you know what day it is?"

"Time doesn't exist here."

"Sir, it is Wednesday. You've been in a coma for almost ten days. We're going to have to run some tests, sir. I will let you rest while we get those scheduled. Perhaps your friends can help to comfort you and put some pieces of the puzzle together for you, yes?"

As Dr. White steps away from Nimitz's bedside to speak with the nurses, Nimitz looks for Ferrol but cannot see him. Ferrol has stepped into the hallway just outside of Nimitz's door and is sobbing quietly. That is where Hayden and Heather find him.

"Oh my god! Ferrol!" Heather rushes to his side. "What is it? Did something happen?"

"He's awake," Ferrol whispers. "He's awake, but he is not making any sense. He's still talking about death and being with her and regeneration."

"What?" Hayden asks incredulously.

"Dr. White is in with him. They're going to run some tests."

"Heather, I'm gonna take Ferrol for a walk outside for some air. While we're gone, maybe you can talk to Dr. White to find out if this is a normal thing."

"Sounds good." She looks at Ferrol and says, "Hey, it's going to be okay, you know? We got Benji back. It'll be okay."

"What if he's not Benji anymore," Ferrol wonders aloud as Hayden gently puts his arm around him and guides him down the hall.

"Oh, Ms. Parker," Dr. White greets Heather as he is coming out of Nimitz's room. "I was just thinking that we needed to talk."

"Of course."

"I would prefer we speak further down the hall if you don't mind so as not to disturb Mr. Nimitz any further. Is that alright with you?"

"That's fine."

They walk a little ways down the hall and duck into a small alcove for some semblance of privacy.

"As you know, Mr. Nimitz legally designated that you be allowed access to his medical records and, if necessary, the legal right to determine any course of medical treatment should he not be capable of doing so himself."

"Yes."

"That being the case," Dr. White explained, "I would like to advise you that Mr. Nimitz might have suffered some brain trauma during his accident after all."

"You said there was nothing wrong with him. You ran tests. You did scans. There was no swelling, trauma, or bleeding. Now that he's out of the coma, you're saying that there might be?"

"Ms. Parker, we did everything that was necessary to assess the damage at the time. And you are correct. Our tests showed no other injuries or traumas. However, now that he is responsive, Mr. Nimitz is exhibiting signs of disorientation, confusion, and delusion. He is talking about death as if it were a person. A woman, to be exact. He is convinced that he died. He canno..."

"He did die," Heather interrupts.

"Pardon?"

"He did die. He was electrocuted and was dead for six minutes. It would have been longer had it not been for the fact that the accident caused the power to go out in his entire building and his neighbor is a fireman. He was dead, though. He's not delusional about that."

"I understand that, ma'am, but he appears to believe he has been dead this whole time."

"He died for six minutes and he's been in a coma for almost ten days. Isn't that reason enough for him to be, what'd you say, delusional, confused, and disoriented?"

"To a certain degree, yes. However, most people respond to questions logically, even if they are still confused on the when and how. For example, in most scenarios, I can ask a patient who has just come out of a coma if they remember what happened that caused them to be taken to the hospital and they will have some idea of what happened. I can ask if they know where they are or what day it is and I will get a logical answer. Mr. Nimitz does not remember what happened to bring him here. When asked if he knew what day it was, he told me that time doesn't exist here. These are not standard response by any stretch of medical science. That causes me to believe there was something the tests missed. Either that, or something new has developed."

"Oh my god," Heather said as she sank against the wall. "What do you need? From me? To do? How do we help him?"

"I would like to run another set of scans. He will need to remain here for the time being until we know he is able to be discharged without any further concerns."

"Yes, of course, anything."

***

The room is dark. Outside his door, Nimitz can hear the standard bustle of the hospital night shift, but nights are much quieter than days. It's raining outside. His curtain is opened enough for him to see the rain drops on the window glass and hear them lightly tapping against the surfaces outside. His television is on but muted. He isn't paying any attention to it. It's just on to keep him from feeling so alone and isolated. It's been almost a week since he woke from the coma. All of his tests have come back with no signs of trauma. They had a therapist come in to talk to him to determine if the accident had caused some latent mental illness to activate within him. He had jokingly thought to himself that Ferrol should be the one analyzing him, but Ferrol hasn't been back to see Nimitz since he woke up. Woke up. Nimitz wonders why comas are talked about in terms usually relegated to sleeping. Comas should have their own terms, not borrowed ones, since they are so unique.

Nimitz continues in this cycle of thought. He wonders what it will be like to resume his life when he is discharged the next day. Part of him wants to go back to his Eternity, to his Death, to something other than this. He's spent the last week having everyone convince him that his death and his Death were all just the delusions of a traumatized brain and nothing more. Having that kind of truth leveled at him made Nimitz feel hopeless and foolish.

A flash of light from the television draws his attention. His eyes fall across the word on the screen and he scrambles to grab the remote and unmute the set.

"...crossing over live on the next Deathhunter!"

"I told you that you and he were connected somehow."

Nimitz jumps when he hears a voice speaking within the room. He scans the room to find the body attached to the voice, but is unable to see anyone in the darkened corners. "Who's there?"

"Over here, darling," the voice calls his attention to the chair next to his bed. The voice is familiar and Nimitz instantly realizes who it belongs to. Death appears in the chair. She looks different, though. Used to seeing her as a lithe, black woman smartly dressed in demure fashion, Nimitz almost doesn't recognize the creature before him. Death is more androgynous now. Their skin is paler, more of a caramel color than the deep black of his love. A neat pantsuit has replaced the dresses and skirts. Their lines are more thin and sharp. The beauty, though, is still there. So is the connection.

"Are you really you? And really here? I've been told that I'm delusional," Nimitz half jokes.

"I'm me. You're you. I'm really here and I am really Death. You're not delusional. You're just privy to an experience that most living humans will never have," Death explains, smiling warmly at Nimitz. He reaches out a hand to them and they remind him quickly, "Same rules apply, Benjamin. Do not touch."

"You look different."

"You're no longer in love with me," Death says with a touch of sadness.

"What? Why would you say that? Of course I am. I'm just confused as to what's really happening to me."

"Maybe I can help to sort some things out. What's confusing you?"

"If I died, then why am I here now?"

"You did die. For six minutes, you were dead, but a fireman revived you. A neighbor of yours. He found you after the electrocution caused the power to go out in your building. He was searching for the cause of the power outage to make sure there wasn't a fire. Your close proximity to him is what saved your life. He got to you relatively quickly and was able to get your heart beating again and get an ambulance to you in time. You are here now because your life was saved."

"Was any of it real?"

"All of it was to some extent. While you were dead, you saw behind the veil. You saw what happens after death."

"To some extent?"

"What?"

"You said it was real to some extent. To what extent?"

"Him, for instance." Death motions to the television set. The Deathhunter commercial is long over, but Nimitz understands what is being implied. "The Deathhunter. As you might have guessed from the commercial, he hasn't done his little crossing over trick yet. With him, you are seeing things that haven't happened yet. Dying can have that effect on some people. Have you ever heard of someone having a near death experience or being revived after being declared dead and they claim to be able to see the future or they know things that happened while they were dead?"

Nimitz nods his head in the affirmative.

"That's why. I cannot explain why some people are more open to these things than others, but you and he are both open and, as I agreed with the Council, connected to each other somehow."

"The Council..." Nimitz repeats slowly. "That's real?"

"Yes, that is all part of dying. The Council, determining the manner of the soul, Eternity Rooms, those are all very real."

"I still don't understand why I would be connected to a man that I didn't even know existed and that I had never even seen before."

"That you know of."

"What?"

"The subconscious works in inexplicable ways. Every face you see in a dream belongs to someone that you have seen in your waking life, even if only in passing. The human brain cannot create a face from nothingness. At some point, your paths crossed with his, you saw him somewhere, his show or a commercial for his show were playing in the background. However it happened, you and he are connected. It runs both ways. He's seen you somewhere, too."

"Just because I saw him somewhere? That formed a psychic, deep bond with him?"

"Grief."

"Grief?"

"You lost both of your parents. He lost his wife and child. Shared grief. Maybe for both of you it was strong enough to bond you despite not knowing each other."

"Grief," Nimitz says the word, feels the weight of it in his mouth, and realizes that Death is right. He realizes how he knows Dr. William Peters.

He looks at Death and sighs heavily. "Why am I not in love with you anymore?"

The question is so heavy in his lungs it is smothering him. The pain of asking it causes tears to well up in his eyes.

"Oh, Benjamin, don't be sad about it. It was inevitable. You love another, you just haven't opened your eyes to it yet."

"The old woman...and the young man!" Nimitz exclaims.

"I'm sorry?"

"Remember, in Cairo, I told you the old woman in the marketplace was speaking in English?"

"I remember."

"She was. Only they weren't her words. They were someone else's. And it happened again only I didn't tell you about the second time. I only realized that one since I came out of the coma. In Israel, there was a young man on the sidewalk. He was speaking English. I stood by him and listened. He spoke English, but they weren't his words."

"I know."

"I can't be sure, but I thi...what do you mean you know?"

"I know everything, Benjamin, like the Council. I knew you were in love with me. I knew you would follow me out of your Eternity. I knew you would see the Deathhunter. I knew you would leave."

"So this was all just some elaborate, what? Game? Trick? Delusion? To what end?"

"None of those. It was what it was as it was meant to be. Everything you felt, everything you experienced, everything you encountered was unique to you. In Israel, you finally saw me for what I truly am: death. I told you that the reason you could see me in all my different forms all at once was because you were accepting me for what I was. You were becoming more open than before. I told you that acceptance made you open and being open made you see what you had once been blind to. I also told you that encountering me was something that tended to inspire change in people, to open them up more."

"I don't understand what this has to do with anything," Nimitz retorts harshly, his feelings still bruised.

"Benjamin, don't you see? It has *everything* to do with everything! It wasn't a game, trick, or delusion. It was you learning to trust yourself, to allow yourself to love and be loved, to chase and protect what is important to you, and to know that you are not alone."

"Ferrol and Heather," Nimitz says softly.

"What?"

"The old woman and the young man. They were speaking, but the words belonged to Ferrol and Heather."

"Yes."

"They were here. In this room. Talking about me."

"Yes, they were."

"I was still in the coma, but they were here the whole time. All of them. They took turns sitting vigil over me. They never left me alone."

"They never left you alone."

Nimitz sits in silence with Death for a little while. He is aware that this is only one incarnation of Death sitting with him in the hospital room, that there are thousands if not millions of others all over the world simultaneously at this moment. He takes comfort, though, in the fact that this one remains by his side, in silence, for however long it takes, which would be a little over an hour.

"I was in love with you, wasn't I?"

"With every ounce of your heart, you most certainly were," Death replies with a dreamy look on their face.

"Were you really...?" Nimitz can't bring himself to finish the question.

"Was I really in love with you?" Death asks the question he cannot. "Yes, Benjamin. Yes I was. I still am. Oh, don't be hurt by that. I know you are now worried about breaking my heart because you are not the type to want to hurt someone. You don't need to worry about that. You asked me about my feelings before and I explained to you that I do have them, that I take them in from souls that I harvest. Some souls are so painful, angry, sour, depleted. Others are so wondrous, beautiful, full, and hopeful that I cannot help but feel the strongest feeling for them. I was not lying when I said that you were the first to ever see me in such a form, so beautiful and elegant, so worthy of respect and appreciation and not fear and repulsion. I watched you, allowed myself to feel you as you moved through your life. I felt the warmth of your friendships, the esteem of your clients, and the profound grief over the loss of your parents, the happiness you held for your friends' successes. I fell in love with you and all that you are even though I knew that it could never be any more than a fleeting moment."

"What happens now?"

"I go back to my realm and you remain in yours."

"I don't even know where to begin..." Nimitz sadly proclaims.

"My dearest Benjamin, if you only look back to what happened, you will be able to clearly see what is to come if only you open your eyes to it. You already know." Death faded before his eyes, their voice trailing off softly like as if from a great distance it was being heard. A great warmth filled Nimitz as he drifted off to sleep with Death's words in his head.

***

"You didn't have to come to get me," Nimitz tells Hayden as he is wheeled to the entrance of the hospital.

"Are you serious, Nim? Of course I did!"

"I could have gotten a car or a cab."

"Don't be ridiculous."

"I just feel like you have all spent too much time taking care of me recently. It's time I get back to taking care of myself."

"There's plenty of time for that. Besides, I'm not gonna hang around. I'm gonna drop you off, make sure you got everything you need, and then I will leave you to your thoughts."

Nimitz gets into the car as Hayden puts his bag in the trunk. His friends had been kind enough to bring him some creature comforts while he remained in the hospital: some of his own clothes, some reading material, and his own toothbrush. Nimitz is extremely grateful for all they had done, but he is still reeling from the revelations of the past week. He is having a hard time believing that he is no longer in love with Death, that Death is no longer with him, and that he is not actually dead. The thoughts feel strange in his brain as he knows most other people would be dropping to the ground and kissing it if they were to be brought back from the dead. Nimitz, however, only feels the loss of a world in which he finally felt fully immersed, completely in his own skin, and vibrant.

"What's going through your mind, Nim? You seem pretty deep in thought over there." Hayden's concern at this point seems almost fatherly as though Nimitz is a fragile child that needs to be handled gingerly. His tone of voice grates on Nimitz's nerves.

"I'm not fragile," Nimitz says out loud.

"What? I know that, Nim. I never said you were. Is that what you think all of this is? You think we are all doing this because we think you're fragile? That you can't take care of yourself? Well, then, let me put your mind at ease: we're not. Do you even understand what you mean to me, Jackie, and the kids? To Heather and Jeanne? To Dean and Ferrol? You're family, a part of us. We were all devastated at the thought of losing you. We love you. All of us do. We realized how easy it would be to lose you, to lose any one of us, and it changed us. We're trying to show you, in the best way we know, how thankful we are that we didn't lose you, how precious you are to us, how sorry we are that we never showed it in the first place. It's not pity, Nim. It's love."

"It changed you," Nimitz quietly repeats.

"Hell, yeah, it did! Shit, I went and got a complete physical because Jackie freaked out. I know that doesn't have anything to do with being electrocuted, but losing someone, even for only a few minutes, opens your eyes. Jackie got a mammogram. Jeanne proposed to Heather. Dean! Shit, Nim, Dean confessed that he gets a little lonely being the confirmed bachelor playboy! Dean! And Ferrol! Ferrol confessed that he's, well, that he might be in love with someone special. It definitely changed us. Opened our eyes to what we had and what we could lose. I think it made us slightly better people."

Nimitz hears Death's voice in his head. *I also told you that encountering me was something that tended to inspire change in people, to open them up more.* He smiles and says, "Jeanne proposed and I missed it?"

"Shit, yeah, about that...pretend I didn't tell you that because they realized that you might be upset that you missed it considering they've known you longer than they've known any of us, so they are planning a redo. So act surprised, okay?"

Nimitz laughs to himself, "Sure thing." He looks out the window and watches the buildings go by as they move towards his apartment.

***

His first evening back in his apartment, in the life he left behind, is difficult. The electric kettle is gone, but the outlet behind it remains as a burnt testimony to what happened. It is a mocking reminder that he had died there while trying to make tea for Death. *Tea for Death. Sounds like the name of an Agatha Christie novel,* he thinks and scoffs out loud. His friends had come while he was in the hospital and cleaned out the fridge, taken out the trash, and made sure that everything that needed to be taken care of was so he doesn't have to worry about spoiled food or roaches. There is some consolation in that since he does like to keep a tidy space. Hayden had taken him by D'Agostino's for some groceries before he left. Nimitz isn't hungry, can't remember the last time he was, but he knows it will come soon.

      He goes into his bedroom, undresses, and takes a hot shower. He stands under the water for some time just allowing himself to break down under the weight of it all. He places his hands against the wall, bracing himself, as his whole body shakes with waves and waves of sobs. He cries for his friends and what they must have gone through. He cries for himself and what he feels he lost. He cries for Death and what it must be like to be death. He cries for their love and how it never had a chance to endure. He cries for all of the souls he witnessed being harvested. He cries for his parents. He cries the hardest for his parents. And before he collapses, he cries for Dr. William Caleb Peters, the Deathhunter, and Vivian and Caleb.

The next morning, Nimitz places a few phone calls and secures an appointment that will prove to be one of the most important he will ever make in his life.

He leaves the house shortly after one o'clock, stepping out into the brisk October air with a determined brow. He decides to walk despite the distance because he wants to feel the air, the smells, and the sounds, all of it against his skin again. He feels reborn after the evening's catharsis and has a new appreciation for what he has endured, experienced, and been gifted. He takes it all in, good and bad. He pauses momentarily at a park where there are kids playing, relishing their effortless laughter, imagining their futures. He hands out money to every homeless individual he passes. It isn't much money, but it's something. He embraces one woman who is so overwhelmed by his simple human gesture that she cries. He stops two men from fighting with nothing more than respectful reasoning and a polite tone. Today, Nimitz is a force of good traveling down the streets of Manhattan.

He arrives at his destination and, for the first time, feels some trepidation at what he is about to do. He makes his way to the elevators, arrives at the correct floor, advises the receptionist who he is and who he is there to see, and takes a seat in the lobby. He doesn't fidget or thumb through any of the magazines provided. He just waits and reminds himself why he's there, what's at stake. He knows he will only get one chance.

"Mr. Nimitz?" the receptionist calls out.

"Yes?" Nimitz replies as he walks towards her desk.

"You can go in now. Last door on the right. He's aware that you are here."

"Thank you."

Nimitz starts down the hall, pausing at its entrance to steel his nerves and take a deep breath, and opens the door. There is a man seated behind a desk. The entire office looks more like the dorm room of a research-minded college student as opposed to a highly pedigreed psychiatrist. There are journals, textbooks, religious tomes, newspapers, clippings, photocopies, and drawings on almost every surface visible. Some of them look familiar to Nimitz and he smiles a secret smile to himself.

"Mr. Nimitz, is it?" the man behind the desk asks.

"Yes, sir. Benjamin Nimitz," he extends his hand.

"Nice to meet you, Mr. Nimitz," the man accepts the offered hand and they shake. "I'm afraid you'll have to excuse me as I don't understand fully why you're on my calendar."

"I'm here to discuss your current line of research and your plans. I believe I might have some insight that could change things for you."

"Well, I can't say that I'm not intrigued. Please, have a seat. Forgive me, but I must ask, have we met before? You look familiar to me, but I can't quite place it."

Nimitz looks at him and smiles broadly. "We have met before, Dr. Peters. It was brief, but apparently I made enough of an impression that you remember my face all these years later. Years ago, you shared an office with a friend of mine, a psychiatrist by the name of Ferrol Toussard. You and I met in passing one afternoon while I was in the waiting room you two shared. I was there to meet Dr. Toussard for lunch. He was still in with a patient, so I was seated. You had a new patient who was a no show. You had come out to the waiting room to see if he had arrived and you initially mistook me for him. We made some small talk after the mistaken identity was cleared up until Dr. Toussard was ready to leave."

"I remember that. Wow, that was a while back. Are you still in touch with Dr. Toussard? He was a good man."

"I am. Saw him just last week. He's doing well."

"That's not why you stopped by, is it? You're not trying to use that to somehow get tickets to the show or some shit like that are you?"

"No. I'm here to try to convince you to cancel the show, change your plans, and save yourself from yourself."

"That's pretty ballsy of you, man. To walk in here like this and make those kinds of statements. Save myself from myself? Fuck you. Who the hell are you to say that shit to me?" William picks up the phone to call security.

Nimitz reaches across the desk and presses down the switch, cutting off the call. "Just hear me out. I don't want anything from you. I will make my case and you can do with it what you will. Once I speak my peace, I will leave without argument and never bother you again. Deal?"

William looks Nimitz in the eyes, sizing him up. Deciding that he is not really a threat, William hangs up the phone, sits back down, leans back in his chair, and says, "Deal."

"In a few days, you will host a show in which you will, as your ads have been putting it, cross over live. During that show, your volunteer Dave, will die."

"How do you know his name? That is confidential and has not been released to anyone! The only people who know it are...did Jakey tell you? Nah, Jakey wouldn't do that. Who could've...the goddamned lawyer? Or Daniel? I swear to god, I will kill whoev..."

"Dr. Peters. Please just hear me out completely. I will explain how I know this, all of this."

"Okay, but I still plan on asking them who ratted."

"Do what you will. Just let me finish. Where was I? Oh, Dave. Of course. Dave will die during that show. You will cross over. You will see glimpses of the afterlife. You will survive and Dave will die. Fueled by your successful crossing over, you will mount another show in which you will not use a volunteer. Instead, you will go under yourself. During that show, your manager will die."

"Jakey? If I'm the one going under, how does Jakey die?"

"Heart attack. Unrelated to that show, but one could guess the stress of the first show's outcome probably plays some part in his demise. You will lose your show after that. The network will deem it too much of a liability. You will go on to mount your show yourself online using handheld cams and microphones and social media. You will travel the world researching how to capture and kill death itself."

"Sounds like, despite everything, I seem to come out alright."

Nimitz is mildly disgusted by William's hubris. He reminds himself what he knows about William and continues. "You will succeed in many respects. You will crack the code of how to cross over. You will enter Eternity more than once. You will see Death. You will see Death's companion. You will capture them both, briefly."

"Whatever you're selling, man, I'm buying," William sits up right in his chair and leans forward suddenly very interested in what Nimitz has to say.

"You will capture Death. Then you will die."

"Well, that took a nasty turn," William jokes. "Seriously, man, is this what you came here for? To tell me some bedtime story that's supposed to make me see the error of my ways, teach me a lesson, and turn me into a good little boy? It ain't gonna work, man. I make a living digging around in people's brains. You can't dig around in mine."

"Do you want to know how I know all of this will happen?"

"Sure. Enlighten me."

"Because when you next see me, I am in Eternity. And when you capture Death, I am the companion that you also capture."

"Okay, now I wanna know what the fuck drugs you're on because this is some far out shit. I've been studying NDE's for two decades, Mr. Nimitz, and I have got to hand it to you, this is the best story I've ever heard. Is there anything else?"

"All those years ago, back in the office you shared with Dr. Toussard, I met you. We had a pleasant conversation. Then I left for lunch with my friend. He told me about you. He told me about Vivian and Caleb."

"Now you just hold on right there, you son of a bitch! How dare you bring them up!"

"He told me how he could hear you sometimes, through the walls, after hours when you thought no one was around."

"Shut up! Shut the fuck up!"

"You would wail. You would cry. You would beg their forgiveness."

William crosses from behind the desk towards Nimitz, his face red with fury. Nimitz does not stop talking.

"You do the same thing the last time I find you in Eternity, when you see them again."

William stops instantly, his right fist balled up and pulled back, his left fist gripping Nimitz's shirt at the collar and holding him. Poised to hit him, William freezes and listens to Nimitz.

"You find them and beg their forgiveness just like you've done so many countless nights in that old office and probably many places since. I was told that you and I were somehow connected and it took me so long to figure out how: grief. We were both connected through our grief over people we lost that meant so much to us, people we felt were stolen from us, and people that we felt were far worthier of this life than we are. You felt that it should have been you that died that night. Not Vivvie and Cay."

William looks into Nimitz's eyes and blinks back tears. In a hoarse whisper, he asks, "How do you know those names? No one knows those names."

"I know them because I heard you talking to them. In Eternity. You've mourned them, William, but you've never allowed yourself to grieve them. You've cried. You've begged forgiveness. You've done everything except sit with your dead, grieve them, and allow yourself to move forward. Instead, you've shielded yourself with work, imagining that you are doing the world some great service by tracking down death and killing her. Death cannot die, William. You can, though. So can Dave and Jakey. Quit while you're ahead. Save yourself. That's how they forgive you. By you forgiving yourself."

Nimitz slowly steps away from William who is still motionless. He picks up his coat and heads towards the door.

"Mr. Nimitz?"

"Yes?"

"Her?"

"What?"

"You said 'her'. You said 'tracking down death and killing her'. Death is a 'her'?"

Nimitz shakes his head in exasperation, smiles, and says, "I've already explained this to you once before in another realm. It doesn't really matter. Goodbye, Dr. Peters."

***

Nimitz washes his dinner plate and sets it out to dry. He leaves the kitchen and pauses by the dining room table, lightly touching the back of the chair where Death had been sitting when he came home that night. He realizes that he misses her, but as he knew her, not as they are now. That thought intrigues him. He moves into the living room and sits down in his favorite spot still with that thought in his head.

He wonders about William, what choice he will make. Before he ever went to his office, Nimitz vowed to himself that he would not pursue it beyond the one meeting. He does not search it online to see if the show has been canceled. He avoids the tabloids. He knows eventually he will discover what William did, if anything, with the information he was given. For now, though, Nimitz is content to remain ignorant of the outcome. He remembers what the Council told him about interfering with the living and he laughs to himself. Still, there's something nagging him and he can't figure out what it is.

He goes to sleep. It is what feels like the first real sleep he's had since this whole thing began. The first real sleep of his life after waking from the dead. His dreams are vivid, lucid, like they're alive themselves.

He moves through the world at Death's side. She is once again the beautiful woman he fell in love with. Her dark skin almost silver in the moonlight. Her dancer's build. Her dark, almond shaped eyes. He hears the old woman in the Cairo marketplace. *I'm in love with him.* He sees the fleur de lis tattoo on the young man in Israel. *He never could have broken their hearts. He has to know that. It bothers me to think that he doesn't know that. They would have loved him no matter who he chose to love.* He is standing with Death on the beach in Maine. He sees his mother and father standing on the porch of their beach house. They wave to him and Death. They're happy that he's found someone who loves him as much as he loves them. He hears Death. *My dearest Benjamin, if you only look back to what happened, you will be able to clearly see what is to come if only you open your eyes to it. You already know.* He sees the fleur de lis tattoo. He sees him mother and father. They're happy that he's found someone who loves him as much as he loves them. Them. Him. He loves him.

He sees the fleur de lis tattoo. He hears Ferrol. *I'm in love with him.* He is standing with Death on the beach in Maine. He sees his mother and father standing on the porch of their beach house. They wave to him and Death. Nimitz turns around to finally kiss Death. As he explodes into stardust, he gazes down to see Ferrol standing on the beach. Asher and Lida are with him. They are all smiling and waving up to Nimitz.

Nimitz wakes up and sits up in his bed in the dark.

He hears Death whisper in his ear, "I told you that you already knew."

***

The entire event is simple. They don't want to make a big affair of it all. They just want close friends and family there to mark the occasion. More of a party, really. The venue is some place special for all of them. They have had dinner there once a month for the past ten years. It's not the fanciest place in Manhattan, but it is the most meaningful. It's the place they've always met at to share their lives, to continue their friendship.

The restaurant's usual lighting has been turned off in favor of a multitude of candles. So many candles, in fact, that Lester, Nimitz's neighbor and life-saving fireman, is not only in attendance as a guest, but also there in case the whole place catches fire. There are bouquets of fresh flowers on every table. Some of the tables have been pushed aside to create an aisle that leads from the entry to the back wall of the main room. Flower petals adorn the aisle, complements of Hayden's three daughters who are tickled to be part of a wedding. They constitute the entirety of the wedding party.

"Dearly beloved friends and family, I have been asked to keep this brief and free of too much cursing." That gets a laugh out of everyone. "If you would have told me a few years ago that I would be officiating the wedding of these two, I would have, well, I can't really say what I want to say because I promised everyone I wouldn't cuss. I came into this fold in a highly unorthodox manner as we all know. It truly was the saving grace of my life that I did. So, I am honored, humbled, and completely ecstatic to be standing here before you all to celebrate Benjamin Asher Nimitz and Ferrol Andres Toussard as they exchange vows and become husband and husband."

Everyone cheers.

From somewhere they hear, "It's about damned time!"

Dr. Peters quips, "Hey! If I can't cuss during this, nobody can!"

The rest of the evening is the most wonderful kind of blur as Nimitz and Ferrol enjoy the love all around them. Heather and Jeanne, who married two years prior, are passing around newly acquired sonogram pictures of their baby. Jeanne is six months along. Jackie and Hayden celebrated their twentieth anniversary earlier this year. Their oldest, Samantha, will be heading off to college soon. Dean and his girlfriend, Adrienne, have been going strong for three years now. Later tonight, Dean will ask her to move in with him permanently. She will say yes. William, the Deathhunter, walked away from his show shortly after his meeting with Nimitz. He has gone back to psychiatry. He has helped a lot of people process their grief and manage their anger over loss.

Nimitz knows that life will not always be as beautiful and happy as it is tonight, but he also knows that, no matter what happens, he will always be open to the experience.

Manufactured by Amazon.ca
Acheson, AB